Frederic Jesup Stimson

The Residuary Legatee

The posthumous jest of the late John Austin

Frederic Jesup Stimson

The Residuary Legatee
The posthumous jest of the late John Austin

ISBN/EAN: 9783337399474

Printed in Europe, USA, Canada, Australia, Japan

Cover: Foto ©Andreas Hilbeck / pixelio.de

More available books at **www.hansebooks.com**

THE RESIDUARY LEGATEE

Or, The Posthumous Jest of the late John Austin

BY

F. J. STIMSON
(J. S. OF DALE)

NEW YORK
CHARLES SCRIBNER'S SONS
1888

CONTENTS.

SCENE FIRST—THE WILL.

SCENE SECOND—THE CODICIL.

SCENE THIRD—THE ADMINISTRA-TION.

SCENE FOURTH—THE FINAL AC-COUNTS.

SCENE FIFTH—THE RESIDUARY BEQUEST.

Scene First

THE WILL

I.

ULYSSES AND PENELOPE.

ON the morning of August 14th, in this last summer, Mr. Austin May alighted at the little Cypress Street station of the Boston & Albany Railroad, and, accompanied only by a swarthy and adroit valet, and a very handsome St. Bernard dog, got into the somewhat antiquated family "carryall" which awaited him, and drove away. May was a stranger to the man in charge of the station, as well as to the wide-awake trio of boys who made it a sort of club, their exchange of gossip, and pleasure resort ; and thus his arrival was unnoticed and unrecorded, though his last absence had extended over a period of several years. It was a most oppressive day ; and what few human beings were dressed and stirring made haste to get beneath the dense foliage, or to plunge into the numerous private-paths and short-

cuts, with which the suburb of Brookline is
provided ; leaving the roads and their dust
undisturbed, except by the sedate progress
of the old carryall, which left behind it, sus-
pended in the air, an amazing quantity of
the same considering its speed, and quite
obscured the morning sun with its golden
cloud. Austin May might have been an entering circus procession, and no one would
have found it out. Even the boys at the
station were sluggish, and indisposed to
"catch on " behind every train, much less
to give their particular attention to one un-
distinguished stranger, with or without a
dog.

May lit a cigar, and the carryall and its
occupants lumbered along unheeded. The
road was walled in and roofed over by a
dense canopy of foliage borne by arching
American elms ; and through its green
walls, dense as a lane in Jersey, only mo-
mentary glimpses were to be had of shaven
lawns and quiet country-houses. When
they came to a gate, with high stone posts,
topped by an ancient pair of cannon-balls,
the carryall turned slowly in. A moment
after they had passed the screen of border

foliage, May found himself in the midst of a wide lawn and garden, open to the sunlight, but rimmed upon all points of the compass by a distant hedge of trees, so that no roads, houses, thoroughfares, or other fields, were visible. In the centre of this stood, with much dignity, an elderly brick house, its southern wall quite green with ivy. In front of it was a large pavilion, some hundred yards removed, low and stone-built, rising without apparent purpose from the side of an artificial pool of water, rimmed with rich bands of lilies. May looked anxiously for the pavilion, and, when he saw it, sank back in his seat with a sigh of relief.

The carryall stopped before a broad, white marble step at the front door ; and the Charon of the conveyance, known locally as " the dépôt-man," having dumped the one leather trunk upon the step, stood looking at the stranger contemplatively, as if his own duties in this world were all fulfilled.

" How much ?" said May.

" Twenty-five cents," said the dépôt-man.

May pulled out a half-dollar. " No matter about the change," he added, as the dé- ˎ pôt-man hitched up his vest, preparatory to fishing in his cavernous trousers for the requisite quarter.

The dépôt-man changed his quid of tobacco, and drove off without a word, the downward lines from the corners of his mouth a shade deeper, as if he profited unwillingly by such unnecessary prodigality, which aroused rather contempt than gratitude. May waited until the carryall had quite disappeared in the elm-trees, and then rang the bell. Apparently, he expected no prompt answer; for he sat down upon one of the old china garden-seats, which flanked the door, and rolled and lit a cigarette. After a few minutes he rang again, louder; the unwonted tinkle reverberated through the closed house, and an imaginative man, putting his ear to the key-hole, might have heard the scuffle of the family ghosts as they scurried back to their hiding-places. At last an uncertain step was heard in the hall, and after much turning of keys and rattling of chains, the door was slowly opened by an old woman, who blinked at the flood of sudden light which poured in, rebounded, eddied, and at last filled each corner of the fine old hall.

"Mrs. Eastman, I suppose?"

"That's my name," said the woman, in a strong down-east accent.

"I am Mr. May," said he.

The woman glared at him as before, and did not compromise her dignity by a courtesy. "Mr. Eastman got your letter," said she, "and I have got your room ready. Will you go there now? I don't know who's to carry up your trunk."

May's valet solved that difficulty by shouldering the leather receptacle and carrying it up himself. The room was large, airy, and neatly kept. A straw matting was on the floor, covered here and there with well-worn rugs; and from about the windows came a twittering of birds. All in it indicated, not a new and modern house, but the well-worn nest of a family that had been born, had cried, laughed, played, made love, and died, in every room. Yet there was no evidence of recent occupation; the room was innocent of those last touches which are the pride of the feminine housekeeper; curtains, splashers, anti-macassars, were few; and no twilled, frilled, or pleated things infested the windows, and impeded the entry

of the outer air. May opened the door of
a large closet ; it was empty, save for a
broad, white, chip hat of prehistoric fash-
ion, and ribbons of faded rose-color ; but,
if it had belonged to a daughter of the
house, it was evident that its owner was
either dead or married, and her womanly
activity was exercised in other locuses and
focuses. No other manifestation of what
Goethe (impatiently) calls the "eternal
woman" was present ; and May's expression
almost approached to a smile as he opened
the door of the spacious bath-room, and
noted the naked mantels and marble slabs,
unencumbered by china dogs, translated
vases, and other traps for the unwary. On
the shelf was a noble pile of rough and
manly towels, and as he turned the faucet,
he found that the water was copious and
cold. From all this you may infer that Mr.
Austin May was a bachelor. I have com-
mitted myself to no such statement as yet,
and May himself would have been the first
to term your curiosity—at the present stage
of your acquaintance with him—an imperti-
nence. As he turned away from the bath-
room the smile of satisfaction died away

upon his lips. Mrs. Eastman was still standing at the door, the incarnation of the custodian, in iron-gray rigidity of dress, and equilateral triangularity of white *fichu.*

"Everything seems to be all right, Mrs. Eastman," said he, graciously. (Behold how simple are the needs of man—give them but fresh water, space, and peace, and their desires are filled ; while womankind—are otherwise.)

"Everything *is* all right," broke in Mrs. Eastman, like the offended Vestal deity, at a statement implying contrary possibilities. Then again she congealed.

May looked at her more closely, with a slight shade of annoyance. How was he to get rid of this woman ?

"You must have had a sadly lonely life here, Mrs. Eastman," said he, by way of placation. And lo ! the flood-gates were loosened and the tide poured forth. Who ever could have suspected Mrs. Eastman of gregarious instinct ? As well have fancied her loquacious. As Moses's wand upon the rock of Horeb, so an adroit phrase addressed to womankind.

"I have not complained, Mr. May ; and

nobody can say that I haven't done by you
as if it were my own house that I was living
in, and the water-back out of order all the
time, and the pipes freezing all the winter ;
and Mr. Eastman, says he, we must have a
furnace fire, and I say no, it ain't of enough
account for us two old people, and so we
sit by the kitchen stove, and my sister, Mrs.
Tarbox, with her four children and the scar-
let fever, over at Roxbury, and nobody to
provide for 'em, for John Tarbox—says I to
Cynthia when he come up to Augusta from
the Provinces (I come from Augusta, Maine,
Mr. May), he ain't but a shiftless fellow, you
mark my words, says I ; and says she, you
let me alone, Miranda, and I'll do as much
by you, s' she ; an' so it turned out, an'
many's the time I've said to Mr. Eastman,
Mr. Eastman, I must go an' see Cynthia, s's
I, for there she is on her back, with her
hands full of children, an' no one to do for
'em but just John Tarbox ; an' s's he, Miranda, it would be tempting Providence for
you to go with your rheumatism, an' s's I,
I can't help that, Mr. Eastman (he's a member o' the church, Mr. Eastman), I guess
Providence ain't got no more to say about

it than my horse-chestnuts in my dress
pocket, an' I always wear flannel next my
skin ; an' s's I, I'd go, come what may, but
for Mr. May's silver, s's I (I keep it under
my bed, Mr. May, and have slept upon it
every mortal night since I took this house),
an' I know I saw a moth in the best parlor
last week, an' the furniture not beaten since
April ; an' so six weeks gone since I saw
my sister ; an' since there's a foreigner in
the kitchen, s' I to Mr. Eastman, Mr. Eastman——"

"My dear Mrs. Eastman," interposed
May, gently, "I had no idea you thought it
necessary to stick so close to the house.
Now I beg that you will go at once. My
servant will get all I want for dinner. You
and Mr. Eastman must both go, and don't
think of coming back before to-morrow—
haven't you any other visits to pay?"

Mrs. Eastman, who had started at the
" my dear Mrs. Eastman " as if May had
offered to kiss her, admitted, ungraciously,
that her husband's sister lived in Jamaica
Plain. But the foreign valet was, evidently,
still in her mind ; and, after sundry prog-
nostications as to the domestic evils to re-

sult from "that man's" presence in the
kitchen, she finally removed herself, with
some precipitation, only when May, in des-
peration, began to take off his coat. Left
to himself, May resumed his coat, drew a
chair to the window, sighed, and lit a cigarette. Mrs. Eastman's disappearance was
followed by a distant shriek; and shortly
afterward there was a slight scratching at
the door. May opened it, and the St. Bernard dog walked gravely in and stretched
himself by the chair ; a certain humorous
expression about his square jowl indicating
that he had been the cause of the shriek in
question. It was a bad quarter of an hour
for Mrs. Eastman's nerves. Fides was the
dog's name, and his master patted his head
approvingly.

May sat down again, and his eye roamed
over the stretch of green turf, a view
broken above by the huge arms of button-
wood, and canopies of English elm.
Shortly afterward he saw the valet emerge
from a side entrance, and step hastily across
the lawn into the shade of a great hemlock, where he stood, gesticulating wildly.
A minute or two later Mrs. Eastman, in an

Indian shawl and purple bonnet, appeared in progress down the carriage-road, limply accompanied by her lord and master. When she disappeared, with her husband and a red and roomy carpet-bag, behind the avenue of elms, the sinuous oriental emerged from the hemlock, and shook his fist. Silence supervened. The prospect of peace emboldened May to light a large cigar. The valet returned to the house, and no sound was audible but the chirping of the birds, the rustle of leaves, and the dignified and heavy breathing of the hound of St. Bernard.

THE PAVILION BY THE LILIES.

As May was knocking off the last white
ash from his cabaña, his servant knocked
softly, entered, and bowed. Rising, May,
followed by the St. Bernard, descended and
entered the dining-room. Upon the walls
were six pictures, four of which were portraits of persons, and two of indigestible
fruit. The persons seemed to have been
eating the fruit. The portraits were all
Copleys, and comprised, first, a gentleman
in a red coat and a bag-wig; second, a young
lady with a sallow complexion and a lilac
satin dress cut so low that only a profusion
of lace concealed her deficiencies of figure;
third, an elderly scholar with long trans-
parent fingers and sinister expression;
fourth, a nice old lady with a benignant
grin. The eyes of the old lady beamed

amiably down upon the table, where lay a
snowy cloth and a glorious breakfast, con-
sisting of a fish, a bird, a peach, and a pint
of claret.   The genius who had wrought
this miracle disappeared, and May was left
undisturbed.

The fish had gone the way of all flesh,
and the bird had gone the way of the fish,
and the first glass of Léoville was awaiting
translation to the sky of human reveries,
when there was a sound of carriage-wheels
upon the gravel. May started. The glass
of claret crashed untasted to the floor, and
its owner sprang upon his feet and fled precipitately. Just as the door-bell rang, he
escaped from the garden door of the hall
and plunged into a maze of shrubbery;
with a hurried sign to the silent servant as
he passed. Rapidly and circuitously, he
circled back behind the hedges until a successful flank movement brought him to the
main driveway at the point where he remembered Mrs. Eastman had disappeared;
here, by a bold dash he secured the front
lawn ; and a few cautious steps brought
him to the side-door of the large, low stone
pavilion aforementioned.   Drawing a brass

key from his pocket, he managed to turn
a grating lock and entered. The door
closed behind him and was carefully bolted
on the inside. The interior was quite dark ;
but May cautiously felt his way to one of
the front windows, and opening the sash,
turned the slats of the blind to a horizontal
position. Through this he peered, breathless with his run. At the front door of the
house was the same carryall that had
brought him from the station ; but its occupants were not visible. May saw the St.
Bernard dog silently threading his way
through the bushes, his nose upon the
trail ; a minute later, and he scratched upon
the door of the pavilion.

" Hush," hissed May, angrily.

The dog scratched, softly. With an im-
patient imprecation, May opened it ; the
dog had a bit of paper in his mouth. May
snatched it eagerly.

" *Madame d'Arrebocques*" was written upon
it, in the hand of Schmidt, his valet. " *Elle
doit attendre.*"

Madame d'Arrebocques ? May knew no
such person. Madame d'Arrebocques?
Why should she write ? Why had she not

sent her card? Had Schmidt spelled the
name right? Ah! at last he had it, thanks
to Mrs. Eastman's garrulity. This could
be no other than Cynthia Tarbox, the ill-
married sister of Miranda, his châtelaine.
And ill-mannered fortune! they had missed
each other on the way. Mrs. Eastman might
return at any moment. As he pondered,
the carryall moved slowly off; but as it
passed the window, he noted that it contained no other figure than the station-
master. The woman, then, was left behind.

May tore out a card and wrote upon it, in
German, *Sie muss fort!* and handed it to
Fides, the dog, who trotted silently off.
What means Schmidt used, May never
knew; but some ten minutes later, four
children came screaming down the avenue, running and gasping for breath, followed by a thin and wiry woman, robed
in a flapping whitey-brown duster, whose
haste and streaming bonnet-ribbons bore
every evidence of extreme mental pertur-
bation.

Shortly afterward Schmidt himself appeared, in his hands a glass and another

2

bottle of the same claret. By a refinement
of delicacy, the glass was full. "*Monsieur
n'a pas fini son déjeûner*," said he ; and May
took the glass with trembling fingers, but
put it down untasted.

"Schmidt," said he, in French, "it is
nearly midday. You must bring everything here. I dare not go back to the
house."

The valet evinced no surprise, but
nodded and disappeared. Left to himself,
May opened the shutters of several of the
windows and looked out. The side of the
pavilion that was farthest from the house
rose directly out of the broad pond or ornamental lake already referred to. This
was to the west ; the northern was screened
by a dense growth of pines, the southern
contained the entrance door before mentioned, and the eastern façade commanded
the house, which was some two hundred
yards distant across the avenue. May
looked out across the water, which was an
ornamental piece fringed with reeds and
water-flowers. In the centre of the little
lake rose a low round island, which had
a comfortable rustic seat and a soft and

grassy surface. May pressed a small knob in the wall near the window, and coming back from it, took a heavy book from one of the dwarf bookcases that lined the large room. The book was a quarto edition of Burton's "Anatomy of Melancholy;" and immediately afterward the adjoining section of bookcase swung slowly forward from the wall, revealing a descending passage-way. Through this May disappeared, and the bookcase swung itself back into place.

Some minutes later, Schmidt entered, after several knocks, with a large japanned tray. Upon this tray was a small paper of bromide of potassium, two boxes of cigars, strong and mild, a carafe of cognac, seltzer, a large opera-glass, a powerful dark lantern, and a six-barrelled silver-mounted revolver. Fides lay on a mat on the floor; but his master was nowhere visible in the room. Schmidt set the tray upon the table and looked about him. Being alone, it must be confessed that his cosmopolitan face showed traces of surprise.

The whole interior of the pavilion obviously contained but one room; and in

that room Austin May was nowhere to be
seen.   In the centre was a huge long centre-table of carven oak ; it was covered with
dust, and upon it was but one large book
—Burton's "Anatomy of Melancholy."   All
the four walls were lined with filled bookcases, and, above them were serried ranks
of engravings, etchings, drawings, but nothing that was not in black and white.   Most
of these had woman for a subject, but woman always either in her least agreeable or
most unspiritual aspect—Katherines with
Petruchio, Madame de Staels, Harriet Mar-
tineaus, Manon Lescauts, Cressidas, and
Marneffes ; Messalinas, Hecubas, Danaës,
Judiths, daughters of Herodias ; an engrav-
ing of the Appalachian Women's Rights
Association, and a charcoal sketch of Dau-
det's *Sappho.*   And of such as were not real
persons or historical characters, there was
but one common characteristic, namely, that
all were shamelessly naked of body and unspiritual of face.   The sole exception to this
rule stood at the farther end of the room
from Schmidt ; it was a full-sized and mar-
vellously perfect reproduction of the Venus of Milo ; having the cynical inscription

upon its pedestal, "A woman without rights."

Schmidt gave a long low whistle, as he went about the room to examine these engravings ; then he returned to the centre-table, wholly at a loss. May surely had not left the pavilion ; but where was he ? He looked out of the windows, and saw only the pine-grove, the house, the lawn, and the lake. In the centre of the lake was a large fountain, plashing merrily, and shaped like the coronal of some huge lily. As he was watching this, the fountain suddenly stopped ; the water-petals wavered and fell, revealing a small grass island that had been screened by the circlet of playing water. A moment after, he started at his master's voice ; May was immediately behind him, calmly putting a book back in the book-case. It was the Burton's "Anatomy."

"You may go now, Schmidt ; I shall not want you until to-morrow. You will stay in the under part of the house ; and not go out under any circumstances, unless you hear a pistol shot. When you hear my pistol fired you will come out rapidly. If fired twice, you will run to the stable for a horse.

If I want you to do anything, I will send Fides with a note."

Schmidt bowed his comprehension and was about to withdraw.

"Stop," said May, "there is one thing more. You must go to Brookline village and hire a fast horse and a buggy, without a driver; put the horse in the stable, but don't unharness him, and shut the door. You may go." Schmidt went.

Left once more to himself, May examined the stores that had been left hy his familiar upon the oaken table. The inspection seemed to be satisfactory. He then consulted his watch, and found with a start of surprise that it was already afternoon. The watch was an elaborate repeater, giving the hour, minute, and second, the signs of the zodiac, the year of our Lord, and the day of the month. This latter was August 14th, as has been said; the time, after twelve.

May's behavior upon this discovery was precipitate and peculiar. First, he arranged with great care the calcium light apparatus so that it commanded the front stoop of the house; then he carefully closed all the shutters of the pavilion save the one toward the house. By this window he sat, peering through the slats of the blind. The sun, getting into the west, shone full upon the stone front porch ; and May kept still there, watching it, in the silence of the midsummer afternoon.

III.

PAUL AND VIRGINIA.

THUS fortified in a material way against
the approach of any enemy, and exalted in
spirit above the slings and arrows of out-
rageous fortune, the minutes seemed hours
and space and time but mediums of his own
control. When his first pipe was finished
he threw it aside and walked openly out
upon the lawn. The very birds were sleepy,
and the park lay spellbound in the shimmer
of its own warm light. Austin took his
way along the margin of the pool ; it was
studded with white still lilies that lay dream-
ily upon the green water ; great gaudy
dragon-flies hung motionless upon the lily-
petals, like silk-robed ladies in some spotless marble hall.

What was it that gave such interest to
the little familiar pool to him, who had
smoked his cigar by the lotos-pools of Yed-

do's moats, or dreamed these same summer
hours away by the fountain of the Court of
Lions in far Granada? Well enough knew
Mr. Austin May what memory it was that
hung about the place; and he smiled his
mature and mocking smile as he remembered his boyish love. Many times had
they two wandered there, May Austin and
himself, wandering together through crusty
Uncle Austin's strange demesne; his uncle
Austin, her aunt's husband. Old John Austin had married for love a poor and beautiful cousin whose mother had engineered
the marriage against the girl's will; and
they had hated one another very cordially.
Too proud to be divorced, John Austin had
built himself this strange pavilion where
his wife had promised she would never go.
She kept her word faithfully; and he never
went into the house without first sending
in his card. They met in company, and
with the greatest courtesy, and gave their
grand due dinners of sixteen, each at one
end of the long table, with a splendid high
épergne between. Mrs. Austin had taken
May Austin into her lonely bosom, and Uncle John had had Austin May home from

college, where his bounty kept him, and had
given him his taste for claret, and tried to
give his knowledge of the world. And they
used to sit there, he and his uncle, in this
same pavilion, smoking, close hedged in
from womankind. And when the old man
had fallen asleep, Austin would creep out
into the park, and walk there with his
lovely cousin May. And on one summer
day, for all the world like this, he won her
heart, this gay young Harvard senior, all
among the rushes by the lily pool. And
Austin had gone back into the pavilion,
quaking, to tell his uncle, and found the
latter very dignified and dead, a bottle of
the famous Eclipse Lafite close by his el-
bow. As with the old French poet

> " Hear ye, who are soon to die,
>   What Villon did before he started—
> He drank one glass of Burgundy ;
>   This he did ; and then, departed."

the claret had not been wasted ; its very
last glass had been savored by its master
before his spirit took flight.

Austin May was overcome with horror.
He ran and gave the alarm at the house,

and then sought his cousin May, whom he found, standing lovely, in the twilight by the lilies. He kissed her, preliminarily, and put his strong arm about her slender waist ; then he broke the news to her, and then he kissed her again, by way of peroration.

Now May Austin was shocked ; but not so much so as if she had seen her uncle since her aunt's death, which had happened some three years before. He had suffered —even commanded—that she should go on living at the house ; but since then, there being no covenance requiring his attendance at the family table, he had lived, eaten, and drunk, entirely in the pavilion. Miss Austin had had a fancy that she had seen him groping about in the shrubbery from time to time, and spying at her through the leaves ; but upon the only occasion when she had gone to see him—it was to thank him for some birthday present, distantly conveyed—he had most mysteriously disappeared. But, as if he appreciated her visit, and were doing her all the honor possible, the fountain played its highest— an almost unheard-of thing since Mrs.

Austin's death. When she had been alive,
the fountain had always played while she
was walking in the garden. Uncle John,
though prejudiced, was always courteous.

But the next memory was clearer yet to
Austin May; and even now a twinge of sadness, as he recalled it, spoiled one puff or
so of his fragrant cabaña. For it was by
this same lily pool, a few days later. Uncle
Austin's remains had been duly disposed of,
according to the terms of the will, and he and
pretty May had met for the last time ; the
last time for a few years, he had said ; the
last time forever, as she had feared. Austin, indeed, had rebelled at this, and spoken
boldly of renouncing everything ; but she
had persevered, and made him see that it
was best, at least for a trial term of years,
for him to comply with his uncle's last be-
hest. And so he was going abroad ; and
she walked with him, by the lily - pool,
through the lawn, through the hedge to the
little seat beneath the linden that had been
her favorite ; and there they had said good-
by, with kisses and tears ; and the same
grim station-master, messenger of fate ! had
carried him off in his carryall, appropriate-

ly named. "The kisses had been very sweet, but the tears had been superfluous."

May smiled as he thought of this, and, lighting another cigar, went back of the pavilion. There he threw back a drawer in the carven oak-table and drew out the queer old will. It was nothing but a copy, bearing the lugubrious skull and cinerary urn which form the seal of the Norfolk County probate court ; but it was already yellow with time, and as May turned amusedly over the old leaves the dust dropped from them upon his spotless Poole-built trousers. Ah, a good judge of claret was old Uncle Austin ; a good judge of claret and of other things. May looked at the bottle of the famous Eclipse (he had not yet tasted it, and there is a certain worldly wisdom about claret very inspiring to those who meditate a practical course of action), and began to read. But his hand shook, as he opened the will, and any doctor seeing him would have treated our hero for nervous prostration, or sent him to a faith-healer at the very least.

"In the name of God, Amen. I, John Austin, gentleman, being of sound mind and disposing memory, and a widower, for which I am reverently thankful" (it has been mentioned that Mrs. Austin died some years before) " do make and declare this my last will and testament.

" My body I consign to ashes, and direct that it be duly cremated under supervision of my executors ; my soul I recommend to him who made it, provided that He have not already taken the soul of Georgiana Austin Austin, my late wife, under his same supervision, in which case I reverently pray that it be left to my own disposition.

" I bequeath to my executors the sum of Five Thousand Dollars, and direct that it be expended in the erection of a large white marble monument to my late wife, aforesaid, said monument to be designed after the florid manner of the later Gothic, and to be placed upon my family lot at Mount Auburn, and to bear, besides the name of my late wife aforesaid, but one inscription, viz. : A PERFECT WOMAN.

" I direct my executors to pay the sum of five hundred dollars annually to the niece of my late wife aforesaid, May Austin, until she be married ; and upon her marriage I direct that said sum be annually paid to her husband, for his sole use and consolation.

"I devise and bequeath my bin of Lafite claret, so-called Eclipse, to my nephew, Austin May, together with all my other estate, real and personal, stocks, bonds, moneys, goods, and chattels, wherever the same be found, but subject only to the following condition, namely: I direct my executors to manage and invest all such moneys and estate, save the use of my house in Brookline, Massachusetts, which I give to my said nephew directly; and all the income, rents, and profits of such estate to pay over to my said nephew annually upon his sole receipt; *provided*, that if he marry at any time within eleven years after my death, or before he shall reach the age of thirty-five, whichever shall first occur, then and in that case I revoke all the devises and bequests to my said nephew aforesaid; but direct my executors to deliver such of my Eclipse claret as then remains, to the most prominent Total Abstinence Association which shall then exist in the town of Boston; and all the rest and residue of my estate I devise and bequeath absolutely and in fee to my residuary legatee.   And I have written the name of said——"

At this point in his reading, May heard a woman's laugh.   It seemed to come from the shrubbery close by.   In order to get more light for the will, he had opened the middle slats of the blind toward the trees; so that it almost seemed possible for a tall girl, standing close to the pavilion, to look directly in.   With inconceivable agility, May dropped to the floor, beneath the window-sill, and ran rapidly around the large room on his hands and knees, close to the wall.   When beneath the table where he had left his opera-glass, he took it up, and adjusting it hastily, stood upon his knees, high enough to look through the open shutter in the window toward the house.   Sure enough, he had hardly got the proper focus, when a young girl emerged from the shrubbery and walked down the road.   But she was very young, only eighteen or so, and though admirably pretty, May was confident that he had never seen her before. He watched her until she had disappeared in the distance ; and then, rising to his feet, returned to the reading of the will.   But

first he altered the angle of the slats of the
blind, so that it would be impossible for
anyone standing outside to look into the
room.

"And I have written the name of the said
residuary legatee in a sealed envelope,
which I hereby incorporate as part of this
will and append thereto ; and I direct that
said envelope be not opened, but remain in
the custody of my executors, or of the
proper court, until my said nephew marry,
or reach the age of thirty-five, or until elev-
en years have elapsed from the date of my
death, whichever shall first happen ; and
thereupon my said executors may open
the same and deliver a copy thereof to my
said nephew ; and proceed to pay over and
deliver all my estate, real and personal, to
my residuary legatee therein mentioned.

"And I will explain, for the benefit of
the gaping and the curious, that this I do
that my nephew may profit by my experience of early marriages. For no man should
by law be allowed to choose what woman
shall be his wife until he be arrived at the
age when he may be hoped to have suffi-
cient discretion not to choose any woman at

all." Then followed the appointment of executors ; and that was all.

May laid aside the scandalous old will and began to think.

How he had laughed at the last clause, he and May Austin, as they wandered by the lily-pond that evening! And when she had persuaded him not at once to give it all up and marry penniless, he had tried to make the best of it. If she would not marry him then, what were eleven years? Eleven years—bah! August 14, 1886—why, he would only be thirty-three and she twenty-seven! But she had refused to make it an engagement, refused even to write to him ; and the poor young Bachelor of Arts had gone off to his steamer most unhappily. And that farewell kiss under the lindens! And the letters he had written back—from Liverpool—beseeching May Austin to reconsider her determination! Austin May took another cigar from the box, and smiled pensively.

Scene Second

THE CODICIL

I.

FROM Liverpool Austin May went to London; from London to Paris; from Paris by the special mail to Constantinople; thence to Athens and Alexandria; and thence to Bombay and Calcutta and Hong Kong; and the impetus of his flight had almost carried him over the Pacific and back to America again, but that he held back on the shore of Japan. He travelled in that country, then in Thibet or in Turkestan. Three years were spent by him in the acquisition of strange drugs, curious pipes, and embroideries, wild songs, and odd languages. He lived in Damascus, Samarcand, Morocco, possibly in Timbuctoo. History records not nor does May Austin, how often he wrote to her. But the summer of 1879 saw him alight at the Gare de Lyon, in Paris. The heat and solitude of that city were equally oppressive, and he fled to the nearest coast. That evening he was seated, robed in soft cloth and starched linen, on the wide veranda of the great *Hôtel des Rochers Noirs*, at Trouville.

No one who pines for outdoor life, primitive conditions, and barbarism—and May was one of the wildest of these—but must admit that the trammels, conventions, and commodities which so annoy him are, after all, the result of infinite experiments of the human race, conducted through all time ; and as such, presumably, each one was deemed successful when made, and adopted accordingly. No question but that men had flannel shirts before starched linen, women flowing robes and sandals before corsets and high-heeled shoes ; and the prehistoric "masher" knocked down his lady-love with a club before he learned to court her with a monocle and a bunch of unseasonable roses. But all these changes were, at the time, deemed improvements ; and one who has lived three years in Thibet or Crim-Tartary, and arrives suddenly at Trouville, is in a fair position to judge impartially. And it is not to be denied that

May was conscious of a certain Capuan comfort, of an unmanly, hot-house luxury, as he sat before the little table with his carafe of ice, brandy, and seltzer, felt the cool stiffness of his linen shirt, smoked his pressed *regalia*, and watched the ladies with their crisp and colored dresses and their neat and silken ankles as they mounted in their landaus for their evening drive. A full string-orchestra was stationed among the electric lights near by, which dispensed, with much verve, the light-hearted rhythms of the latest opera bouffe ; and beyond the planes and lindens shone the moonlit sea, as if it also were highly civilized, and part of the decoration of the place. May knocked the ashes from his cigar as who should say, " I, too, am a Parisian of the nineteenth century ; " quaffed a few sparkles from the iced carafe and bottle, and pretended to be interested in the latest Faits-Paris of *Figaro.* He was beginning to realize the delights of youth and riches and free travel ; he had been nothing but a school-boy in America, and a sort of wild man since.

And as he so sat, there came to a table next him two people, and sat down. One

was a middle-aged man, with an iron-gray
imperial, a tight white waistcoat, and the
rosette of the legion of honor at his button-
hole.   The other was the most beautiful
woman he had ever seen.   She was dressed
in the most delicate and languorous cloud
of violet and gray, strengthened here and
there by black lace ; no ribbon, jewel, or
flower was on her lustrous black hair, or
about the soft and creamy neck ; and she
was evidently much absorbed in what her
companion was saying, for May could see
that she clinched her fan in her hand that
was beneath the table until the delicate
ivory broke.   They talked very rapidly, in
French ; but May, whose acquaintance with
unknown oriental dialects was so manifold
and various, knew hardly French enough
"to last him over night." And it is of es-
pecial importance that one's French should
last over night.

Whatever they were saying, they were
reiterating it with continually increasing
force.   The man in the tight frock-coat began hissing it between his pointed teeth,
and the pretty woman crushed the last
fragment of the fan to ivory slivers on the

floor. At last, the gentleman rose, and with a *pardieu* which even May's untrained ear could recognize, upset a champagne glass, and strode hastily away ; the lady eyed him until he disappeared, and then drooped her long lashes, and hid her eyes in her pretty hand. Her bosom rose and fell convulsively, and May's chivalric heart beat sympathetically in the same time. Suddenly her deep eyes opened, and opened full on Austin May's.

"Sir," said she, in English, "you are a gentleman—save me!" Save her? Aye, Austin May would have saved her from the devil or the deep sea, and with no thought of salvage. All he said was, "Why, certainly." It afterward occurred to him that he should have said, "Pray, command me, madam." But this seemed to satisfy her, for she unbosomed herself directly.

"I know I may trust an American," said she. "Listen—I will confide to you my true name. That man—that *mouchard*—with whom you saw me, sinks I am ze Comtesse Polacca de Valska. Well, I am ze Comtesse Polacca de Valska. Now you know all."

Unfortunately, Austin May knew very little. But evidently the Comtesse Polacca de Valska was a personage of European reputation. He bowed.

"What can I do?" said he, earnestly. "Madam de Valska has but to command." (This was better.)

"Hist!" said she, mysteriously. "Polacca de Valska—never mention ze name. Eet ees a spell, in Poland ; even now my noble Polacco languishes in Siberia ; but in France, in Russia—eet ees a doom. Say zat I—say zat I am your compatriot—Mrs. Walkers—anysing." And the nerve which the unhappy countess had shown throughout the interview suddenly collapsed. She burst into tears. As she dissolved, the American congealed, all the blue blood of Boston rigid in his veins. When the little Frenchman appeared, May offered his arm to the countess ; and together they swept proudly to the door of the hotel.

"*Arrêtez,*" cried the Frenchman. "*Connaissez-vous*—do you know, sare, who it is ?"

"It is my friend—my friend, Mrs. Peter Faneuil, of Boston," said May, with a readiness that charmed him at the time.

" *Mais, monsieur*——"

" Do you dare, sir, to——"

May glared at him for a moment, and the latter recoiled, like any Frenchman, before his Anglo-Saxon attitude. They entered the hall of the hotel ; the countess pressed his arm convulsively in her gratitude, her heart too full for words. " *Merci, chevalier,*" said she, simply. May's heart bounded at the compliment, and with satisfaction that he understood her French. " I have a carriage here," said she ; and they found the elegant landau still at the door. ·

" Where shall we go ? "

" I will tell you later," said she.

May got in, and a footman closed the door of the carriage. The liveried coachman whipped up the horses, and the pair rolled forth into the darkness of the summer night.

At this point in his recollections, May looked at his glass of claret and re-lit his cigar ; and though he did not know it, this was precisely the course of action that had been adopted at the time by the Frenchman with the rosette. He drew his chair up to the table where the countess had been sitting, with a slight shrug of his padded shoulders, and more imperturbability of manner than would have flattered the valiant defender of oppressed beauty, had he been there to see it.

But at this period May was whirling along in the countess's carriage, through the darkness of the night, close by the sea-beach and the pale shining of the long, slow surf.

II.

THESEUS AND ARIADNE.

THE next morning May rose after a sleepless night, and wandered pensively along
the beach. His head was full of the Comtesse Polacca de Valska; perhaps a drop
or two of that charming personage had
brimmed over from his head into his heart.
Their romantic drive had ended in no more
romantic a locality than the railroad station ;
there he had parted from her, perhaps forever. For she had assured him that after
her meeting with the rosetted Frenchman
the air of Trouville would not be good for
her, and she had taken the night mail for
Paris. Her maid was to follow on the next
day with luggage. As soon as she was
safely established, and had, at least tempo-
rarily, thrown the enemies of her unhappy
country off her track, she was to let May
(her deliverer, as she entitled him) know,

and he could see her again. But, alas! as she tearfully remarked, that might never be. The French republic was now seeking to curry favor with the despotism of the Czar, and even Prince Obstropski had had to leave Paris for Geneva. Austin wanted to kiss her hand as she departed, but feared lest this trivial homage should jar upon a heroine like her. The bell rang, the guard cried out; one last glance of her dark eyes, and all was over. She was gone, and May felt that perhaps the most romantic episode of his life was ended.

He went back to the hotel, but, unfortunately, none of the famous Eclipse claret was at hand. So he contented himself with brandy and soda. Visions of nihilistic fair ones, of Polish patriots and *Italia irredenta* kept him wakeful through the night. For the Comtesse had told him of her Italian descent, of her alliance with the great patriot Milanese house, the Castiglioni dei Cascadegli. . . . And the Count Polacco de Valski was immured for life in the Siberian mines. . . . Poor devil! May cut another cigar, and reflected upon the Count's unhappy condition.

In a few days he received a letter from
the countess. It was a mere line, incident-
ally telling him that she had not established
herself at Paris, but at Baden-Baden ; but
it was principally filled with pretty thanks
for his "heroic chivalry." The expression
had seemed a trifle too strong at the time,
even to Austin May.

But when he arrived at Baden-Baden,
and saw how charming the countess was in
her now elaborate *entourage*, he made allow-
ances. Man is generous by nature, espe-
cially to beautiful heroines with husbands in
Siberian mines. May thought of the hap-
less Polacco de Valski as turning out poly-
form lead-pencils by the ribboned bunch,
and marking them BBBB, and then, alter-
nately, HHHH. May had been much exercised in mind how to explain his sudden
trip to Baden-Baden, and had devised many
plausible reasons for going, all of which
proved superfluous. The countess did not
seem in the least surprised. He found her
weeping over a letter. "See," said she, "it
is from Serge."

"The d—— Really ?" said May.

The countess folded the letter, kissed it,

and replaced it in her bosom. This was an extremely embarrassing proceeding to May, and he kept some time silent. With his Anglo-Saxon awkwardness at social comedy, he thought that Polacco might as well be kept out of the case.

"Shall we go for a drive?" said she, at last.

"Delighted," said Austin May.

The drives about Baden-Baden are charming. You wind for miles upon the brows of castle-crowned hills, overhanging the gay little valley; and then you plunge into the ancient gloom of the Black Forest, and the eerie pines, and a delicious shiver of wildness and solitude, all the time with the feeling that the Kursaal and its band are close at hand, should the silence grow oppressive. There, if your heart do trouble you, you can look at pretty women; and, if the eternal verities beset your spirit, gamble for napoleons.

The countess drove two little cream-colored ponies, and encouraged May to smoke his cigarette most charmingly. . . . . Bah! why go on with it? Even now, over the Eclipse claret, May could not but admit *that* he had spent in Baden-Baden three of the most charming weeks of his life. He would not mind passing three such weeks again, could he be sure they would be *just* three such weeks, and that they would end at the same time. But, *que diable!* because the play is amusing, we do not wish to stay in the theatre forever. And May nervously glanced at the window, as he thought he heard the sound of carriage-wheels again. He had smoked too much strong tobacco, probably; but, after all, it was even now only the middle of the afternoon—not sunset, or near it. He might have to come to stronger drugs than tobacco, to stronger deeds than tobacco-smoke, ere the evening was over. Hence that arsenal with which he had provided himself.

Well, to cut it short, he fell in love with her. Of course he did. He adored her. Possible! He wanted to marry her. This seemed impossible; but he had most certainly said so. He was barely twenty-five, and she—well, she was older than he was. And she had a husband in the Siberian mines. As May looked back upon it, this seemed her only advantage. But, after all,

4

it was her patriotism that first attracted him
—her heroism, her devotion to her unhappy cause, or causes. Italia irredenta! Poland! Nihilism! For May was not quite
clear which one or more of these was chief
in her mind ; and nihilism was a new word ·
then, but it sounded dangerous and at-
tractive. Could he not be her chevalier,
her lieutenant, her esquire? It was no
more than Byron had done for Greece,
after all. He was free, independent (for
the next eight years)—broken-hearted, he
was going to add, but stopped. After all,
May Austin had not refused to marry him ;
and three of the eleven years were gone.
At all events, there was nothing to prevent
his attaching himself to a forlorn hope, if
he chose. Eight years of chances were in
his favor ; and at the worst—if neither May
Austin got married, nor Polacco died—he
could make a rescue of the husband from
Siberia and do the BB pencils himself. He
lay awake many nights thinking of these
things, and at last he was emboldened to
speak of them to her.

How well he remembered the day he did
so! The day—but no, it was evening.

They had driven out after dinner, (did any
man ever propose before breakfast ?) and
the scene was a moonlit glade in the Black
Forest. The two ponies stood motionless ;
but their fair owner was much moved as
he poured into her delicate ear his desires
and devotions. It was so noble of him, she
said, and was moved to tears. And then
his devotion to her unhappy country ! and
she wiped away another tear for Poland or
Italia irredenta. How she wished Serge
could have met him, and could know of
this ! And she wiped away another tear
for Serge. But no, my noble American—
noble citizen of a free country ! It could
never be. Poland and she must bear their
woes alone. They could never consent to
drag down a brave young Bostonian in their
wreck. And then, how could she ever reward him ? With her friendship, said Austin. But the Comtesse seemed to think
her friendship would be inadequate.

The scene was becoming somewhat oppressive ; and May, at least, was conscious
of a certain difficulty in providing for it a
proper termination. In the excitement of
the occasion, he had felt emboldened to

take one of her hands, which he still re-
tained; the other was holding the reins of
the two cream-colored ponies. He could
hardly simply drop it—the hand and the
conversation—without more; and yet what
suitable catastrophe could there be for the
situation? Might he kiss it, and cut the
conversation? It were a mere act of courtesy, no breach of respect to the absent
Serge. As a boy of twenty-two he had never dared; but as a man of twenty-five——

She did not seem in the least surprised.
Possibly she had thought him older than
twenty-five. But May, after that little ceremony, had dropped the hand most unmistakably; and she turned the ponies' heads
away. May gave a last look to the forest-
glade, as they drove out from it, and reflected that the place would be impressed
upon his memory forever. It was really as-
tonishing the number of places that were to
be impressed upon his memory forever!

A restless week followed. He saw the
Countess de Valska every day; but there
was something uncomfortable in their relations—a certain savor of an unaccepted
sacrifice, of an offering burned in vain.

The countess would not let him seek the Austrian foe on her own behalf, nor yet be-dew the soil of Poland with his blood ; and it was very difficult to say what he was to do for her in Baden-Baden, or, for matter of that, what the noble Polacco de Valski could do in Siberia. Poor Serge !

Yes, poor Serge ! On the eighth day, Austin May, calling on the countess, found her in a lovely *négligé*, dissolved in tears. (He had been refused her door, at first, but finally, after a little pressing, had been ad-mitted.) The countess did not look up when he entered ; and Austin stood there, twisting his hat in sympathy, and looking at her. Suddenly she lifted her head, and transfixed his blue eyes with her dewy black ones.

"Dead !" said she.

"What ?" responded May, anxiously. "Poland ? Ital——"

"No, no !" she cried. "Serge—Serge !"

"Your husband ?" cried he—"the Count Polacco——"

The countess dropped her lovely head in a shower of tears, as when a thick-leaved tree is shaken by the wind, just after rain.

"He has been dead a year and a half," she moaned.

"A year and a half?"

"Nineteen months. He died on the 23d of February, 1877—three weeks after the last letter that I ever got from him."

"But how—but how did you never know?" said May, wildly.

"Was it not cruel? The despotism of the White Czar! Sometimes they would keep his letters for a year, sometimes they would let them come directly. They would not let me know for fear that I—ah, God!" She sprang to her feet with a sweep of her long robe, and shook her jewelled finger at the chandelier.

"Can you blame us that we kill and die for such a despotism, such a tyranny, as that?" Then suddenly, as she crossed by a sofa, she straightened up to her full height, like a wave cresting, poised a brief second, then fell in a heap—a graceful heap—her head resting on the sofa in her hands.

Then the young man had to seek, not to console her, but to calm her, to lift her from the floor, to bring her ice-water, a fan, a feather, pour oil and salt upon the wound, toilet-vinegar, or other salads. May never knew exactly what he did ; but it was like consoling an equinoctial gale. Hardly had she got fairly calm, and sobbing comfortably, and sitting in a chair, and he beside her — and he remembered patting her clasped hands, as one does a spoiled child's —when she would dash upright, upsetting. the chair, and swear her vengeance on the cruel Czar. . . . And at this point in his reminiscences May winced a little ; for he had by no means a distinct recollection that he had not sworn his vengeance on the Czar with hers. And, when you come to think of it, the Czar's injuries to Mr. May cried not as yet for deeds of blood.

III.

DIDO AND ÆNEAS.

MAY repeated his visit of condolence every day for several weeks. At the end of
that time the season at Baden-Baden was
drawing to a close, and it became necessary
that the countess should betake herself and
her sorrowing heart to some other refuge.
May knew this, and it troubled him.

For he now felt that he not only admired
Mme. de Valska as a patriot, but that he
loved her as an exceedingly beautiful and
fascinating woman. Surely, here was the
heroine of his youthful dreams—a life that
were a poet's ideal.

To link himself with her and her noble
aims, to be a Byron without the loneliness,
to combine fame in future history with present domestic bliss—what a career!

He loved the countess, he adored her;
and he fancied that she deigned to be not

indifferent to his devotion, to his sympathy. But — there was the shadow of the late count.

And the countess seemed much broken by his death. True, she no longer gave way to wild bursts of passion ; she never wept; in fact, in Austin's presence, she rarely mentioned him. But there was a sadness, a weak and lonely way about her, as if she could not live without her Serge's protecting arm. It must have been a moral support, as he could have done but little from his Siberian mine ; but, whereas she used to be brave, enterprising, facing the world alone, now she seemed helpless, confiding, less heroic, perhaps, but still more womanly. Austin only loved her the more for that. And it emboldened him a little. After all, her husband had been dead a year and a half, though she had only known of it a few weeks. He determined to speak. Why should his life's happiness—possibly hers—be wrecked upon a mere scruple of etiquette ?

He took his opportunity, one day, when she spoke of Italy. (Now, that the count was dead, she seemed to think less of unhappy

Poland, and more of unredeemed Italy ; as
was natural, she being a Cascadegli.) He
took her hands at the same time, and
begged that she would redeem him with
Italy. His life, his fortune, were at her ser-
vice, should she but give him the right to
protect her, and fight her battles for her always. "I know," he added earnestly, "how
your heart still bleeds for your noble husband. But your duty is to your country,
to yourself. And remember, though you
heard of it but yesterday, the Count Polacco
has been dead a year and a half."

"Nineteen months," sighed the countess,
with a sob, going him four weeks better.
And before he left the room they were engaged. He did not go to bed that night ;
but wandered in the moonlight, treading as
on clouds. Favored young man !

In the morning, he noticed with delight
that she had laid aside her long crape veil.
Already, said she, her country called for
her ; she must recommence her labors, and
the deep mourning would attract too much
notice. May had vaguely fancied she would
start at once for Milan or Warsaw, and
after a few months' delay he would meet

her, and they would have a quiet marriage ceremony. But she explained to him that the true arena of her labors was in Paris. Here was the focus of conspiracies ; here she must live and have a *salon,* and call together her devoted countrymen. Here she would need his protection, and, with his American passport, he could safely visit her oppressed fatherland, when events required action on the spot.

Obviously, as he recognized with joy, this plan made it necessary for them to be married immediately. But then he must speak to her of his uncle's will. Not that it mattered much ; he was quite ready to renounce fortune, even life, for her ; but she must know that they would not be rich. It was a mere formality ; but it must be done. So he told her of the curious will ; and how, if he married before August the fourteenth, 1886, he was to lose all his uncle's property, even to what remained of the celebrated Eclipse claret. But then, what was money? Particularly to them, who had no other aims than love and patriotism ; both commodities not to be bought, or measured in sterling exchange or napoleons. But the countess seemed to attach much weight to May's communication.

Money, alas! was in these sordid times necessary, even for patriotic revolutions. The wheels must be greased, even when Bucephalus drew the chariot. Still, this was not the essential. She was quite willing to share her small fortune with the man whom she loved; but how could she bear to ruin him—to make her alliance his sacrifice? Suppose he should ever repent his action? And here May began to make his oaths eternal; but she stopped him. Was there no other way? Could there be no escape, no legal device? Lawyers would do almost anything, if paid enough. But May shook his head, and pressed again her hand to his lips; and her dark eyes brimmed with tears.

She, for herself, would be willing to suffer him as her adorer, to trust him as her knight, her follower, as he once had proposed before. And, by that arrangement, he would not lose the fortune. But what would the world say—the cold and heartless world? And she looked at May imploringly, as if for advice.

And May had to admit, in answer, that
the world would be likely to make itself as
disagreeable as usual under similar circumstances—particularly, now that the unhappy
count was dead, and could no longer defend
his heroic consort from the spite of petty
spirits. The moral support was something,
after all. May had true Boston reverence
for what the world said ; and it never occurred to him that even a heroine, who had
braved two emperors, might brave its ver-
dict.

For some moments neither spoke. What
was there to say ? But the silence grew
oppressive ; and at last she broke it with a
cry.

"Farewell, then," said she.

But at this May broke out with a round
oath. Farewell it should never be. What
cared he for his uncle's fortune, or for. the
estate in Brookline, when his future lay in
Poland? He would have a little left; he
could win more by his own exertions. For
a moment his impetuosity almost overbore
her resistance. But then the Paris *salon*
was a necessity ; and half of her own estate
and all of poor Polacco's had been seized

by foreign despots. She would think it over. She would give him an answer that night. And then there came a lover's parting ; and May went back to his hotel, not wholly desperate, and got the engagement-ring he had ordered, and sent it to her. It was of small diamonds ; but then there was a necklace, sent from Paris, of perfect Oriental pearls. A woman could afford to get engaged once a month, for such a necklace.

And he had gone back that evening, and he had found a letter. The countess had gone, leaving the note behind her. It was edged with deep black ; and May took it now from his pocket-book, yellow and worn, with a smile that would have been cynical had it not been slightly nervous.

" *Très-cher !* " it began, " I cannot bear " (it was all in French, but we will make clumsy English of the countess's delicate phrase, as did May, when he read it now) " that your love for me should be your ruin. It is too late for me to deny that you also have my heart ; I can only fly. Otherwise my woman's weakness would destroy either you or myself. I shall go by the morning train to Frankfurt, where I shall stop two

days. If you do not wish to betray me,
seek not my refuge out. I shall keep the
ring as a pledge" (she says nothing about
the necklace, it occurred to May, at this late
date)—" a pledge that I shall be faithful to
you, as, I hope, you to me. For what are
six or seven years?" (At her age! thought
May, with a shudder.) " I will devote them
to my unhappy countrymen. (*Compatriotes*
was the original, which may be feminine.)
" But wait for me until you are free ; and
perhaps, who knows ? my Italy redeemed !
I will join you, and be one with you forever. Meantime you will travel, possibly
forget me ! But on the fourteenth of August, 1886, you will be at home. *On that
day you will hear from me !"*

May laid the letter down and shuddered.
This was most unquestionably the fourteenth
day of August in the year eighteen hundred
and eighty-six. He seized nervously the
glass of claret; but, as he raised it to his
lips, looked through the blinds, in the direction of the house. His second glass of
claret fell unheeded to the floor.

A carriage was standing before the front
door, and beside it stood a footman in livery.

Scene Third

THE ADMINISTRATION

I.

THE JUDGMENT OF PARIS.

THE three years following May's unhappy affair with the Countess Polacca de Valska had been uneventful. He had not plunged again into foreign parts, but became a student of the barbarities of civilization. He saw what is termed the world, particularly that manifestation of it which attains its most perfect growth in London and Paris. Perhaps it would be too much to say that he forgot the Countess de Valska, but certainly his feelings toward that unhappy fair one underwent certain modifications. And as he was in the meantime in the receipt of some twenty thousand a year from the estate of the late John Austin, he by degrees became more reconciled to the extremely practical view the cruel countess had taken of their duties in relation to that gentleman's wilL

He very often wondered as to who might
be the residuary legatee. It would be a
wild freak, that he was sure of. It was
quite on the cards for Uncle Austin to have
provided that, since his nephew did not
want the money, it might go to the devil for
all he cared—or to the Total Abstinence Society.

It is more sad to say that, as time went
by, certain metaphysical doubts as to the
objective reality of the Cascadegli and the
Siberian mine began to obtrude themselves.
Faith of the most stubborn description remained to him, so far as the countess's
Paris salon and her beautiful self was concerned, but he failed to see the necessary
connection between Trouville, Baden-Bad-
en, Italia Irredenta, and the Parisian police.
And Serge had removed himself, for an en-
cumbrance, in a singularly accommodating
way.

But May was a man of his word; and he
looked forward, at first eagerly, and afterward with mingled emotions, to their promised next meeting in Brookline, Mass.

The woman Byron might have married
was not the wife for Talleyrand. And May's

volcanic or Byronic age had passed, and he was in the tertiary period. Taking her for all she said she was, she wouldn't do in society, and he doubted that she was all she said she was.

However, it gave him no serious trouble until after his acquaintance with the beautiful Mrs. Terwilliger Dehon. Youth has a long future ahead of it, and a young man of twenty-seven easily discounts obligations maturing only in six years. But when May was thirty, and well launched in London society—whether it was the charms of Mrs. Dehon aforesaid, or the vanishing of youthful heroism and that increase of comfort which attends middle life—a political heroine like the Countess Polacca de Valska no longer seemed to him the ideal consort for a man of his temperament.

Young men have their time for falling in love with comédiennes upon the stage ; and then they turn to the comédiennes of real life. Only in the latter case it is to be noted that they ever prefer the heroines of a tragedy.

It was on the very evening before all advice became superfluous, that he confided

his troubles to Tom Leigh, and asked his
advice. Tom Leigh advised him that "he
was in a devil of a hole."

"But what am I to do?" said May. "I
am bound to meet her—in five years."

"Perhaps she won't come," said Tom.
But Austin shook his head. If she didn't
come, there was May Austin—but he checked
himself. He had never spoken of his cousin
to Tom Leigh. She was doubtless married
ere this ; and if she wasn't, he preferred her
to the countess.

"Perhaps her husband ain't dead," sug-
gested the resourceful Tom. But May
smiled, bitterly. "I guess he's dead enough
—much as ever he was."

"Then I don't see but what you'll have
to stand the breach of promise suit," Tom
concluded, with a grin. In these misfor-
tunes, truly, there is something pleasant to
our best friends. We know that Messrs.
Winkle and Tupman must have chuckled
in secret over even Bardell vs. Pickwick.
But the idea was unspeakably awful to our
fastidious hero. Moreover, he darkly im-
agined that the countess had other resources
than a breach of promise suit.

This was on the evening before the hunt; on that epochal brink of their first meeting. And on the next day all this talk became superfluous; as superfluous as for Falstaff to demand the time of day.

II.

MRS. TERWILLIGER DEHON—ah, Mrs. Dehon! Great heavens! why had they not
met earlier—before she had sacrificed herself upon Terwilliger's commonplace al-
tars—before her radiant youth had been
shrouded in tragedy?

The Russo-French police may be successfully evaded, but not so the laws of society.
Naught but misery could he see in store
for them both—one long life-agony of di-
vided souls.

Of course, it took some time before this
dismal prospect lay fairly out before them.
At their first meeting there was nothing
sadder in sight than the purple hills of Exmoor and the clear cascade of Bagworthy
Water; and their talk was broken only by
the cheerful yelp of hounds. And there
had been fortune, too, in this; fortune we

call fate, when fortune turns out ill. He
had hardly seen her at the Cloudsham
meet, and but just knew who she was.
Thither he had gone with his friends, the
Leighs, to see the red deer hunted in his
ancient lair ; and as he stood there, snuff-
ing with his horse the sea-breeze that came
up from Porlock Bay, immaculate in coat
and patent-leathers, she had ridden up
with a fat and pursy citizen beside her.
This stall-fed citizen was horse-back on
another square-built brute, and it was very
Psychecide to call the wretch her husband.
A Diana, by heaven ! thought he ; and, indeed, she sat her horse as any goddess
might, and clothed her own riding-habit as
the moon her covering of cloud.

" Who's that ? " said he to Tom Leigh.

" That's the girl that married old Dehon,"
said Tom. " She did it——"

But when or how she did it Austin never
knew, for just then there was a joyous bay-
ing from the hounds, and whish ! they
scampered downward, skirting hanging
Cloudsham Wood. Unluckily, they were
at the wrong end of the field, and before
they reached the steep bit of gorsy moor

that overlooks the valley everyone else who meant to ride had disappeared in the cover of the forest.   She reined in her beautiful horse on the very brink, and looked up the valley over Oare Hill ; May stood a few yards below and looked down the valley in the direction of Porlock.   Then she looked down the valley to Porlock, and May looked up the valley to Oare Hill.   And their eyes met.

Her beautiful eyes glanced quickly off, like a sunbeam from a single eyeglass. She turned, as if in sudden decision, and sped like an arrow over the high moor. May's eyes followed her ; and his soul was in his eyes, and his body went after the soul.   One dig of the spurs nigh unseated him, as if his spirited horse scorned such an incitement to chivalric duty ; and so, for some twenty minutes on end they rode, May neither gaining nor losing, and both out of sight of the rest of the hunt.   Now and then the cry of hounds came up from the forest-valley on the right, and May fancied he heard below a crashing as of bushes ; but he had faith in his guiding goddess and he took her lead.

The high winds whistled by his head, and there were blue glimpses of the sea and wide gray gleams of misty moorland; but the soft heather made no sound of their mad gallop, and May was conscious of nothing else save the noble horse before him and the flutter of the lady's riding-habit in the wind. Now the earth that rushed beneath was yellow with the gorse, now purple with the heather; here, he would sail over a turf-bank, there, his horse would swerve furiously from the feeling of an Exmoor bog; where she would ride, he would ride. This he swore to himself; but she rode straight, and he could make no gain. At the top of the moor, almost on the ridge of Dunkery Beacon, was a narrow cart-path, fenced six feet high in ferny turf, after the usual manner of Devonshire lanes. May saw it and exulted; this was sure to turn her, till she found a gate at least.

But his beautiful chase rode up the gentle inner incline and sailing over the lane like a bird, was lost to sight upon the other side.

"By heavens!" swore May to himself. "She means to kill herself."

He rode at it and cleared the six-foot
width of lane successfully; but his horse
could not bunch his legs upon the narrow
bank beyond. He rolled down it, and May
over his head into a bank of heather.

The eager American prematurely began
to swear before his head struck the ground ;
and before his one moderate oath was finished, he was upon his horse and off again.
Mrs. Dehon had not even turned round
upon his disaster ; but May was none the
less attracted to her by that. What was
mortal mishap to a spirit wrecked like hers ?
Why should she ?

They were riding down hill now ; and
she was riding a little more carefully, favor-
ing her horse. But May cared neither for
his horse nor his neck by this time. Straight
down the hill he rode ; and by the time
they reached the Lynn he had gained the
quarter-mile he lost. Here she had pulled
up her horse, and he pulled up his at a courteous distance ; and both sat still there, in
the quiet valley ; and the noise of their
horses' breathing was louder than the rustle
of the wind in the old ash-trees around
them.

May wondered if his pilot was at fault ; but hardly had the thought crossed his mind before they heard again the music of the hounds, at full cry ; and far up, two or more miles away, toward the Countisbury road, they saw the stag. Though so far off, he was distinctly visible, as he paused for one moment on the brow of the black moor, outlined against the blue sky ; then he plunged downward, and the hounds after him, and May's horse trembled beneath him ; and May wondered why his goddess was not off.

But instead of riding down to meet the hunt, along the valley of the East Lynn, by Oare Church and Brendon, she turned and rode up in the direction of Chalk-water. May followed ; and hardly had they left the Lynn and gone a furlong up the Chalk-water Combe, when she struck sharp to the right, breasting the very steepest part of Oare Oak Hill. If she knew that he was behind her, she did not look around ; and May again had all that he could do to keep his guide in sight.

And now the event proved her skilful venery. For as they crested Oare Oak

Hill, and the long bare swell of the moor
rolled away before them, the sharp cry of
the hounds came up like sounds of victory
in the valley just below. Well had Diana
known that either way of the Lynn would
be too full of his enemies for the now exhausted deer to take. It must make for
Bagworthy Water. Long ere they had ridden down the Lynn to the meeting of the
streams, the hunt would have passed; but
now, as they looked across and along the
lonely Doone Valley, they saw the full
pack far down at their feet, close by the
foaming stream.

Then May could see his leader whip her
horse, as if she would open the gap between them; and he set his teeth and swore
that he would overtake her, this side the
death. And he gained on her slowly, and
the purple and yellow patches mingled to a
carpet as they whirled by him, and he felt
the springing of his horse's haunches like
the waves of a sea; and below them, hardly
apace with them, was the hunt and the cry
of hounds. Down one last plunging valley
—no, there was another yet to cross, a deep
side-combe running transversely, its bot-

tom hid in ferns. But the hounds were
now abreast of them, below, and there was
no time to ride up and around. May saw
her take it; and as she did, a great shelf of
rock and turf broke off and fell into the
brook below. He saw her turn and wave
him back ; it was the first notice she had
taken of him; and he rode straight at the
widened breach and took it squarely, land-
ing by her side. Then, without a word,
they dashed down, alongside of the slope,
and there, in upper Bagworthy Waters,
found the deer at bay, and the hounds ;
but of the hunt no sign, save Nicholas
Snow, the huntsman, with recking knife.
He had already blooded his hounds ; and
now he sat meditatively upon a little rock
by the stream, his black jockey-cap in his
hands, looking at the body of the noble
stag, now lifeless, that had so lately been a
thing of speed and air. A warrantable deer
it was, and its end was not untimely.

May pushed his panting horse up nearer
hers. She was sitting motionless, her cheeks
already pale again, her eyes fixed far off
upon the distant moor. "Mrs. Dehon!"
said he, hat in hand.

The faintest possible inclination of her head was his only response.

"I have to thank you for your lead," said May.

For one moment she turned her large eyes down to him. "You ride well, sir," said she.

When the M. D. H. and others of the hunt came up, they found these two talking on a footing of ancient friendship. The slot was duly cut off and presented to Mrs. Dehon; and many compliments fell to our hero's share, for all of which May gave credit to the beautiful huntress beside him.

Tom Leigh cocked his eye at this, but did not venture to present him to her after that twenty-mile run. It were throwing the helve after the hatchet, to present the man after the heart. And thus it happened that to her our hero was never introduced.

When Mr. Dehon arrived, some hours later, Tom Leigh led him up. "Mr. Dehon," said he, "I think that you should know my particular friend, Mr. Austin May." And Tom Leigh cocked his eye again.

May looked at the pursy little old man, and felt that his hatred for him would only be buried in his enemy's grave. But his enemy was magnanimous, and promptly asked them both to dinner, which May did not scruple to accept.

6

PERSEUS AND ANDROMEDA.

Austin May fell devoutly in love with Mrs. Dehon. This was without doubt the *grande passion* of his life. And it was hopeless.

He was just at the age when such affairs are sternest realities to modern men. He was beyond the uncertainty of youth, and before the compromises and practicalities of middle life. And there was something about Gladys Dehon to make a man who cared for her ride rough-shod, neck or nothing, over all things else. All the world admired her; would have loved her had it dared. There was no daring about it in Austin's case; his audacity was not self-conscious; he simply followed her as he had followed her over combe and beacon on that Exmoor day.

People could tell him little about her, save

that she had been very poor and very
proud, and was very beautiful. Gladys
Darcy—that had been her name—last of a
broken family of Devon and of Ireland.
She had neither sister nor brother, only a
broken-down father, long since sold out of
his Household captaincy. She had sold
herself to Terwilliger Dehon, the rich specu-
lator ; and she was his, as a cut diamond
might have been his ; bought with his money,
shining in his house, and he no more within her secret self than he might have been
within the diamond's brilliant surface. And
two months after the wedding her old
father had died and made the sacrifice in
vain. Then she became the personage that
the world knew as the "beautiful Mrs.
Dehon." May used to dream and ponder
about her, long hours of nights and days ;
and he fancied that something about her
life, her lonely bringing-up, her father's
precepts, had made her scornfully incredu-
lous of there being such a thing as the
novelist's love in life. She had been a
greater nature than her father, and all man-
kind had been nothing to her as compared
with even him. Too early scorn of this

world's life prepares the soul for evil compromises.

Her character, her nature, she expressed in no way whatever. She had neither intimate friends, charitable occupations, tastes, follies, nor faults. She shone with a certain scornful glitter of splendor, but even of old Dehon's millions she was not prodigal. She never flirted; she never looked at one man long enough for that. Her one occupation was hunting, and she rode to hounds in a way to jar the nerves of every M. F. H. in England.

Tom Leigh was afraid of her; and when they were asked for a week's visit that autumn, in their box in Leicestershire, refused to go. May went. And if there was a man of whom she was not utterly unconscious, he surely was the one. Perhaps there was something about his way that she liked. For, with neither much speech, delay, nor artifice, our hero made his heart and soul up into a small packet and threw them into her deep eyes; and when she looked at him, he had them; and when she looked away, they were gone. And this he did perfectly frankly and directly, but without spoken

words. The world saw it as clearly as did
she, and liked him none the less for it. He
was quite incapable of any effort to conceal
it; old Terwilliger might have seen it had
he been so minded. Possibly he did, and
the knowledge lent an added value to his
chattel in the old stockbroker's mind. Mrs.
Dehon herself treated May with perfect
simplicity, but with an infinite gentleness,
as the moon-goddess might have looked
upon Endymion.

This state of things got to be perfectly
well known to the world. Such things
always are well known to the world; nothing
is more striking than the perfect openness
with which our heart-histories are revealed
in modern life, except perhaps the ease with
which those most intimately concerned
maintain a polite and unembarrassed appearance of utter ignorance upon the subject. All the world loves a lover, particularly a hopeless one; and it was quite the
mot d'ordre of society that year for people to
ask Mrs. Dehon and the handsome American to their houses together.

And Mrs. Dehon? Well, before the coming of spring she felt a great and trustful

friendship for this incidental castaway upon
the waters of her troubled life.   May afterward remembered that she told him many
things about herself ; and she had spoken
of herself to no one else before, her own
father included.   She even let him see a
little of her heart.   And it is an axiom that
he who sees ever so little of a woman's
heart has but to take it.   Seeing is posses-
sion.   This is the wisdom of the fair Melu-
sine, and other wise old mediæval myths.

It is needless to say that May had absolutely forgotten the Countess de Valska ;
more completely than even she had forgotten the Siberian mausoleum of her Serge.
I May thought of her once in that year, it
was to dismiss her memory with a curse
for his own folly, and a mental oath that no
Trouvillian countess would part him, should
his way ever be clear to Gladys Darcy.   He
would not recognize the hated name of
Dehon, even in his thoughts.

In his despair, he confided in Tom Leigh
again.   Tom saw no reason to change his
previous opinion.   The hole seemed if
anything deeper, now that two were in it.
"I don't see but what you've got to escape

the countess, bring Serge to life, kill old
Terwilliger, and thus give her two years'
mourning," said he. " Why the deuce didn't
you find her out first?" he added, ruefully.
"Old Terwilliger only married her eighteen months ago."

"I don't know," said May. "Why don't
you invent his railway schemes, and dis-
cover his Cornish mines?"

" True," assented Tom. "Old Dehon always does get in on the ground floor. However," he added, brightening up, "if you
can marry her, you'll get her and his money,
too."

" Damn his money," said May.

Tom looked shocked, and changed the
subject, and May's heart continued so to
bleed internally that soon Gladys Dehon's
marble brow would soften to pity as she
saw him wane. Meantime Terwilliger's
capon-lined stomach waxed apace, and even
his digestion was to all appearance unim-
paired.

Now, it is probable that ours is the first
civilization known to history where this
state of things could exist, be mutually
known, and continue in tranquil perma-

nency. But it does—that is, it nearly always
does—and it is a credit, after all, to our
teaching and our times that it does so. The
ancient Perseus cut Andromeda's chains,
and departed with her by the next P. and
O. steamer they could signal ; the modern
one sits down on the strand beside her, and
he and Andromeda die to slow music—that
is, in case either should chance to die before
the malady is cured. And Andromeda's
master relies on the strength of his chains
and on Perseus's good bringing up, and is
not wholly displeased at the situation. Particularly for a sly old stock-broker like Terwilliger Dehon, whose idea of values is
based on the opinion of the street, a Perseus
to his Andromeda is half the fun. The
world, on the whole, approves the situation ;
but the husband Dehon is not a popular
character, and it likes the Perseus better.
Not, of course, that it is willing to condone
anything improper, particularly on the
part of Andromeda.

But Austin May stood the passive rôle for
precisely twelve months ; and then he made
up his mind that something would have to
break. He hoped it might be the neck of old

Terwilliger ; but Providence seldom spoils a dramatic situation by so simple a denouement. And, to tell the truth, considering the way the three rode to hounds, it was much more likely to be his own or Gladys's. One thing was sure : their triangular relations were too strained to continue. He came to this conclusion after one precisely similar day upon Exmoor, a year after their first meeting ; except that upon this occasion the deer took to the sea below Glenthorne and was drowned, and he and Gladys rode homeward side by side in silence.

Accordingly, that night Austin May wrote a letter ; and in the morning showed Terwilliger a telegram from America, took his departure, shook hands hard with old Terwilliger, barely touched the slender fingers of his wife, but, when he did so, left the letter in her hand. May kept no copy of this letter ; but he remembered it very well. It ran as follows :

" GLADYS :

" I must not stay in England any more. I cannot bear it. I know that you are unhappy, and I must go where, at least, I shall not see it.   Nor can I trust myself with you after our ride of yesterday.

"Remember always that, wherever I am, I am always and only yours.   This is a very strange thing to say; but I think there are times when men and women should show each other their hearts, however much the truth may shock the prudes and pedants. And I do very much wish to say that if ever you are free, I ask you to marry me.

"It is a sad thing that the circumstances of your wedded life are such that I can say these things to you and not offend you. But you have shown me enough of your heart for this.

"I go now into Asia.   A trivial duty will call me to my family home for one day, on August 14, 1886.   Then, if I do not hear of you there, I shall disappear again.   After that I shall write you once a year.

"Good-by,

"A. M."

Scene Fourth

THE FINAL ACCOUNTS

I.

Poor Austin! A boy's love feeds on the romance of hopelessness, flourishes apace in the shadow of despair; it delights in patient waiting, in faithful fidelity, in lapses of years; but a man's is peremptory, immediate, uncompromising. Some secret instinct bids a Romeo to contemplate a tragedy with cheerfulness; and ten to one that his years of gloom change, as they fall behind him, to "*un joli souvenir.*" But a man, middle-aged, knows when he wants his Dulcinea, and he wants her here and now. No glamour of blighted affections can make up for the hard facts of life to him

When a middle-aged man can't get the woman he wants, there are three recognized and respectable courses open to him. He works a little harder, plays a good deal

harder, or he marries someone else. The
last was out of the question for a man so
consumed by the fires of passion as Austin
May, but the fuel of his heart was trans-
formed into nervous energy of the entire
system. He plunged again, like a rocket,
into a rapid and circuitous course of travel
and adventure ; and, after a brilliant career
through the remote East, descended, like a
burned-out stick, some fifteen months later,
in San Francisco. Thence he went home.

The fact was, he wanted rest. His heart
was tired of throbbing, his head weary with
thinking. And all his mad adventure had
only tired the body, had made him sleep at
night, nothing more. He had been through
the world again, but Gladys Dehon was all
of it to him. He thought of her now with
a certain dull pain—less madly, more hope-
lessly, than in England the two years before.

He could not bear to go back to his home.
He went to Boston, and he saw his lawyers ;
but he did not go out to Brookline. This
he vowed he would not do until that day
when he had promised Gladys he would
be there. He did not forget that he had

promised the countess, too ; but he was no longer so much troubled by the countess. He would kill her, if necessary.

Meantime, he went to pass the winter in New York. He had himself elected a member of two fashionable clubs. He followed the hounds in Long Island and in Jersey. He went to dinners and he danced at Germans, albeit with an aching heart. He re-naturalized himself ; he made friends with his countrymen, and he studied his country-women. He got himself once more *déso-rienté* in American society. He observed what respect was everywhere shown to the VanDees, and how little, comparatively, one thought of the McDums. He found that civilization was pitched on a higher scale, financially, than he had supposed. Thirty thousand a year was none too much for a man to marry on. Now, Austin had not over twenty thousand, even if he fulfilled the hard conditions of his uncle's will.

He took an interest in yachting, and gave orders for a cutter that was to beat the prevailing style of sloop. He also imported a horse or two, and entered one of them at Sheepshead Bay. He had a luxuriously

furnished flat, near Madison Square. He
went to St. Augustine in the spring, with
the VanDees, and while there was introduced to Georgiana Rutherford. He saw
her afterward in New York, and early in
June he asked her to marry him.

Miss Rutherford was a young lady of su-
preme social position, great wealth, and
beauty. She had for two years been the
leading newspaper belle of New York society. Her movements, her looks, her
dresses, the state of her health, the probable state of her affections—everything about
her, to the very dimples in her white shoulders—had been chronicled with crude pre-
cision in the various metropolitan journals
having pretensions to *haut ton* (for high tone
is not a good translation), and had thence
been eagerly copied throughout the provin-
cial weeklies of the land. Miss Rutherford
was absolutely a person to be desired.

It would not be fair to May to say that he
was false to Gladys Dehon. His passion for
her, too vehement, had fairly burned itself
out. In the two years since he had left her,
May's heart had, as it were, banked its volcanic fires. However fissured were its ra-

vined depths, the surface was at rest, and the lava-flood that concealed it was already cool. And a beautiful huntswoman who had ridden out of sight of her first husband, as had Gladys Dehon, was not at all the sort of person for middle-aged Austin May to marry and bring to Boston. These things he felt for some weeks before he proposed to Miss Rutherford, and she was precisely the sort of girl he saw was best. If old Uncle Austin had selected her himself, he could not have made a better choice. And well, thought May, he saw the motives of his kind old uncle's will, and the wisdom born of much experience, and long consideration and a knowledge of Eclipse claret that had prompted it. A young man, if left to himself, would choose him a different wife for each three years of his life. It is only after he has run the gamut of all impossibilities that he settles down upon the proper thing. And this, at last, May felt assured that he had done.

May did not pretend to himself that he loved Georgiana Rutherford as he had loved Gladys Dehon. Even now, he was not blind to that. But he thought that she was pretty,

7

and well-placed, and good style; and she had a large fortune, and a still larger family connection, all of the very best securities.

In fact, May, at least so far as he admitted to himself, did not do justice to the qualities of Miss Rutherford. Miss Rutherford was a very charming girl; much cleverer and much better educated, to say nothing of her style and beauty, than any embryo Gladys Dehon that May had ever seen. She was perfectly mistress of her own heart, as she was of her own fortune, and it was danger-ous to present to her foreigners, lest they afterward shot themselves. They always went wild about her; much to Miss Ruther-ford's discomfort. Some would besiege her; others would curse her; others, still, say evil things about her in the true Parisian manner. Miss Rutherford remained "more than usual calm " through it all.

She had the reputation of being a flirt, but it was not so. She tried her adorers, Portia-like, successively; the moment that they failed to reach a certain standard, it was entirely right and fair for her to drop them. Some of them would cry that they were hurt, and these she contemned from her very soul. She did not regard such matters as subjects for tears. Marriage was a step in life, like any other, and only deserved more serious consideration because it was final.

This was the woman whose love was to make heart-haven for Austin May; the serious, sober choice of his manhood, after all his boyish follies were past. He had told her very seriously and politely of his desire to marry her, one Sunday evening, on the piazza of a house at Newport. It was necessary for him to speak in a low tone, as the people of the house were not far off. She was silent for some seconds, and then he had kissed her.

But here came in the first really difficult thing to do in the whole proceeding. Not, indeed, the kissing her. But how was he to tell her of the countess and Gladys Dehon? And yet he must tell her, if only to explain the necessary delay in announcing their engagement. He looked at her in the light that came from the late sunset; how perfectly of the great world she was! He could not bear to lose her now; she was just such a wife as he would invent for himself, had she not existed. She was sitting silently, in a pose that was full of grace and training; much too finely bred to be blushing because he had kissed her. No man had ever kissed her before; and yet, when she deemed that the occasion had come when she could fitly let one do it, she no more blushed because she had so resolved than she would blush at entering a ball-room.

Then he pulled himself together, and told her very calmly the history of his life. She was greatly interested, and listened with attention and sympathy.

"Of course, you must be there—on August 14th, I mean."

"And keep my word?"

"That," said Miss Rutherford, "I must leave to you. You can't keep your word with both of them."

"After all," said May, hopefully, "they may not come."

"You surely do not expect them to cross the Atlantic in person to meet you?"

"Oh, no!" said May. "They won't do that—but they may write or telegraph." But May did not feel sure what Mme. Polacca de Valska might or might not do.

"At all events," said she, "I think our engagement had better not come out until after the 14th of August." And May felt constrained to admit that this was best.

"And I do not think that you had better see me until then."

"What?" cried Austin.

But Miss Rutherford was firm. She would not have him with her every day unless she could tell people that they were engaged. What was she to say to the world if, after that 14th of August, he were to be engaged to Mrs. Dehon, for instance? This she delicately hinted; but, moreover, she told him she had promised to visit the Larneds, at Pomfret, and the Charles Mt. Vernons, at Beverly, and to spend three weeks with the Breezes, at Mount Desert, in August. He could not trail about after her; and it was only three months, after all. So May had consented, with an ill grace; and when she left, two days later, he found nothing better than to join VanKnyper on a yachting cruise. Then he had gone up on the Restigouche, salmon-fishing; and on the 12th of August he was in the Maine woods.

II.

THE IDYL OF ANTEROS.

In the leisure of the forest, Austin May reflected—for the first time comprehensively—upon his conduct of life. It seemed to him that the only sensible action of many wasted years was his getting engaged to Georgiana Rutherford ; and yet, for the moment, it rather added to his perplexities. He felt convinced that Tom Leigh would say it put him in a greater hole than ever. Here was he engaged to three women at once, and all the engagements matured upon the fourteenth day of August proximo. Why is it that there is not such a thing as the making an assignment for the benefit of one's heart's creditors ? He might then place himself in the hands of some respectable chaperone as assignee, and pay each of the contracting parties thirty-three per cent. Or he might even get a composition, or an

extension at long time. Possibly the other
two would assign their claims to Georgiana. If she were the sole creditor, he fancied that they might effect an arrangement.
She certainly had the only lien on the few
remaining assets of his hard-worked ventri-
cles.

Georgiana Rutherford! What a perfectly civilized creature she was. How well
she would look at the end of the state din-
ing-table in the Brookline house, with the
épergne in front of her. Then how grace-
fully she would sweep out, at the head of
the procession of ladies—Brookline ladies,
with a guest or two from Boston or Jamaica
Plains—and leave him and his friends to
their bachelor-talk and cigars. But first,
after being married, he had promised to
take her up the Nile. May had already
been up the Nile.

May slipped off the rock into the rushing
river. He had got to thinking, in the absence of salmon, and forgotten his where-
abouts. It was clumsy of him, he reflected, as
his boots queaked soddenly campward. He
was getting heavy, and slow, and middle-
aged. And suddenly he felt a yearning for

the wilds, for wilder wilds even than Aroostook County. He had been now for six
years in high civilizations—Japan, India,
England, or, at worst, the States. There
were several dreams of his scheming-time
not yet effected. Among others, a trip
from Hudson's Bay, in canoes, through the
Great Slave lake to the Pacific. He was
almost on the ground, with good guides
and an outfit ; why not start at once ? But
there was the fourteenth of August next to
come, he reflected.

A strange wagon was in the camp when
he got back ; a single buckboard from the
nearest settlement, and it bore a pretty
girl. May had conversation with her. A
veritable Lady of the Aristook was she ;
not over-idealized, like the heroine of Mr.
Howells. Really, she had a certain rudi-
mentary charm. Suppose, thought May,
I were to make her my dusky bride ? For
dusky, read freckled.

By Jove, thought May—an idea indeed.
If he gave it out as such ? If, in consideration of a trip to Boston, new bonnets, and
a junket of quite Merovingian dimensions,
she were to consent to go to Brookline and

personate his bride, for that day only? How natural that he, at the very end of his eleven years, should have plunged into nature and married la première venue. It was just the thing, he felt assured his friends would say, that he was certain to do. Why, even the heroes of the Lady of Aroostook did as much. And even the Comtesse Polacca dei Cascadegli de Valska could have nothing to reply to such a living argument as this Maine girl would present. My wife— Mrs. Austin May. Gladys Dehon would scorn, but believe. And then, having nobly earned her reward, his salvatress might retire to her primitive forest decked with new fal-lals to astound the rustic breast.

But now, confound it, here as always, the cursed conventions rose in his way. The proprieties were ever his fatality, a very ghost of Banquo at the feast of life. Why had he been born in Boston? True, they had once saved him from the countess; but now they were to offer him a humble sacrifice to her unlovely years. For she came first chronologically, and she was certain to come first in fact.

May had no further ideas; and he had to

leave his river at the height of the salmon season.

We have told how, on the 14th of August, he arrived at Brookline, true to his appointment with all three. He got to Boston late in the evening before, went to his club, passed a sleepless night, and took an early morning train for Brookline, as we have seen.

And, perhaps, as we have also seen, a much more awkward thing than this had happened. Austin May was there, ready to meet any one of them. The period of probation required by the will had elapsed.

But as May travelled up to the city in that hot weather, he had been wondering to himself which and how many of them he should see, and it had become very clear to him that he did not feel the least desire to see any one of the three.

His uncle's will had well been justified. With shocked shamefacedness he thought of the countess, that Trouville heroine that he believed to be little better than an adventuress, a gambler, tracked by the police. And Mrs. Dehon—well, if Mrs. Dehon were to ride madly up that quiet Boston lawn,

May felt sure that he should flee in terror. And Georgiana Rutherford—now that
it came to the point, and after his three
months' consideration, May did not feel
that he wished to marry even Georgiana
Rutherford.

He gave little thought to his impending
doom, still less thought of escaping it. He
was as one who had been released eleven
years upon parole, and must now give himself up to be shot. He even gave himself
little curiosity as to whose the fatal bullet
would prove to be. A man ordered out
with a file of soldiers to be executed looks
upon the levelled row of muzzles with an
absolute impartiality. He was in the position of the celebrated d'Artagnan, who, having three duels in the Pré aux Clercs, and
certain of being killed by Athos at 12, gave
himself little anxiety about Porthos, who
was to follow at 12.15, or Aramis, who was
only due at 12.30.

But, as the day wore on, and the reaction
followed the artificial strength given by
many cigars, his state of mind had approx-
imated to an abject and unreasoning terror. And in this mood he was, late in the

afternoon, when he turned and saw, stationary before his front door, that carriage, with its footman in livery.

His one instinct was to conceal himself. Nervously he grabbed the heavy "Burton's Anatomy;" the secret door swung open; the fountain in the lake began to play, and in a score of seconds May was hiding in its cool and watery depths.

III.

THE UNCERTAIN GLORY OF A NEW YORK GIRL.

WHEN May emerged in the little grass island, screened safely by the play of falling waters, he was breathless with the run ; and his heart pounded against his ribs with the violence of his emotions. The countess it unquestionably was. None but she would arrive in open carriage and pair and splendid livery. And May reckoned he would have to stay there, in the shelter of the fountain, until the light made his escape safe and possible. As for seeing her, that was out of the question. Had he still cared for Mrs. Dehon, he might have choked off the other one ; but he had not pluck for it now. He had mildly hoped that Gladys and the countess might have arrived at the same time and settled it between them ; but Allah had willed otherwise. It was damp and uncomfortable upon the little island, however, without even a cigar; and he did not dare go back to the pavilion.

As he stood peering through the falling water the carriage turned about, left the house, and came down the driveway. May was astounded. He tried his best to see who was in it, but the distance was too great. He fancied that he made out a figure upon the back seat, but it was that of a young man. He was surely too young for Serge; but, possibly, Serge had left a son. This, indeed, was extremely probable. And the son was gone to the gate to await more formal introduction to his papa-in-law; and had left the countess in the house.

This was the most terrible possibility that had yet occurred to his fevered imagination, overwrought with suspense and too much tobacco as it was. For a moment the idea of the buggy and the fast horse in the stable presented itself as the only certain means of escape. But at the same instant he saw Fides emerge from the side door, carrying something white in his mouth. The hound came to the door of the pavilion and scratched there; not finding any response, he took to coursing around the building, in wider and wider distances, until his circle included the whole pond. When he had once more made the circuit of this, without getting trail of his master, he lifted his nose from the ground to give utterance to occasional lugubrious howls.

This was impossible. Something must be done at once, or his chief retreat would be discovered. May rapidly descended through the subterranean passage, and appearing at the door of the pavilion, whistled softly. The dog bounded toward him, and May took the letter from his mouth. It was accompanied with a card of "Mr. Burlington Quincy," as May hurriedly read. Now, Mr. Burlington Quincy bore a name utterly unknown to Austin May.

He looked at the note. It was certainly not in the handwriting of Madame Polacca de Valska, and May breathed a sigh of relief. He opened it.

"My dear Mr. May: (it began)

"I know you will not misinterpret my action, when I write to tell you that our en-

gagement cannot be made known to-day.
The bearer of this, Mr. Burlington Quincy,
of Boston, I did not know when our pleasant acquaintance began last year, but I
feel sure that he is the only man I have
ever——"

"Loved," added May to himself, mechanically, as the first page came to an end.
Without troubling himself to read any
further, he merely looked at the signature,
which was, "yours ever sincerely, Georgiana
Rutherford."

"Bah!" said Austin to himself again, and
he crumpled up the letter and threw it
upon the pedestal of the Venus of Milo.
A very different sort of girl from Georgy
Rutherford, she looked at him with an air
of dignity offended by his flippancy. Certainly a great weight was off his mind, even
if it did leave behind the faintest conceiva-
ble smart of irritation. One, at least, was
disposed of satisfactorily, and he threw himself into the great arm-chair with a sigh of
relief. He wished Miss Rutherford joy of
her bargain, though he could not but think
it ill-bred of her to choose the replacing
victim as the messenger of his release. The

only man she had ever loved, indeed! And who was Mr. Burlington Quincy? Well, it mattered little to him.

May looked at his watch; it was seven o'clock. Only five hours more of this awful day remained! His condition was one of absolute nervous prostration; and he looked in a glass to see if his hair had yet turned gray. Could it be that they would none of them appear? He felt almost hungry, but that eating was out of the question for one in his position. He could, however, take a biscuit and a glass of claret; and this he did.

But May was fated that day to have hard luck with his uncle's wine. Hardly had he begun to sip the glass, when a loud knocking at the very door of his pavilion made him drop it, and again seek refuge in his fountain hiding-place. From there he looked through the jets of water and saw that the knocker was none other than the faithful Schmidt.

May hastened back again to the pavilion and opened the door.

"What do you mean by this?" said he, angrily. "Did I not tell you not to come

8

out under any circumstances, unless you heard a pistol-shot ?"

But, alas ! The effect of the solitude, the heat, and the excitement of his master's strange behavior had been too much, even for the perfect valet. Moreover, he had felt it his duty to finish all his master's so precipitately abandoned bottles, lest they should fall into the hands of the enemy. If Mr. Schmidt was not tipsy, it was clear that he soon would be. He had been leaning heavily against the door, and as his master opened it suddenly, he fell into the room, head over heels to the floor; and there, without getting up, he endeavored to bow apologetically, and swayed to and fro with the effort, smiling a meaningless smile and holding a visiting-card in his right hand. May took it mechanically. It was edged in deep black ; and upon it he read the simple legend :

Mrs. Terwilliger Dehon.

IV.

MAY grasped the half-drunken valet by the coat. "And you let her in?" said he.

"I said, m'sieu'," gasped out poor Schmidt, "that m'sieu', was here."

With a groan of mingled rage and terror, May flew to the door and made it fast. Then he took Schmidt by his offending coat and shoved, rather than led, him into the subaqueous passageway. When they emerged upon the island, May said, with a final shake :

"Now, sir, go and tell all the world that I'm not at home—d'ye hear? And come back and tell me ; and that you may come back sober, I'll clear your thick head for you." And suiting the action to the word, May hurled poor Schmidt through the cool jets of the fountain ; and he disappeared with a startling plunge in the waters of the

ornamental lake. They were but a few feet
deep, however, and Schmidt scrambled to
his feet and went wading through the lily-
pads to the shore. And in a few moments
he came back, still wet, but quite sobered, to
the brink nearest the island.

"What does she say?" cried May.

"That she will wait for M'sieur," came
back the answer that May heard; and he
sank upon the rustic seat with a feeling that
all was over with him. Should he still fly?
He could not bring himself to break his
word at this late hour. If it could be that
the widowed Mrs. Dehon had come all this
distance—unwomanly as it was—he could
not leave her now. Moreover, it was exactly
like her. She was just the woman to take
the leap herself, rather than trust herself and
her heart-secrets to written words. And as
May pulled himself together and went toward the house he wished he could have
conjured back one spark of that flame he
once felt for her. His crusty old uncle
had not foreseen that thus, by the rash
heir's promise, the wise provisions of his
will could be evaded. What would his
wise uncle have done in a similar situa-

tion ?—Ordered a monument at Mount Auburn and prepared the remains for it afterward, perhaps. His head was too cloudy to think.

May reached the doors of the house. It was already dark ; and he had one last moment of hesitation as he pressed his hand upon the carved-oak door-knob. Then, with a rally of his sense of honor, he turned it and entered the house.

The great hall was quite dark ; and Austin had to feel his way to the dining-room, into which, as being the only habitable apartment, Schmidt had had to show the fair Gladys. Here was a single candle burning ; and beyond the remains of what was evidently Schmidt's dinner, just under the Copley portrait of the lady in the lilac dress, sat a solitary figure.

But May started back as he saw it. It certainly was not Gladys. It was—it was a man ; and as it rose and came forward to the candle-light there appeared unmistakably the red face and pudgy figure of her elderly husband ! For a moment the joyous reaction held May speechless ; but then he sprang forward.

"Mr. Terwilliger Dehon, I am delighted to——"

But Terwilliger waved him back with the gesture of an M.P. quelling an assembly of constituents ; and in his hand he carried a letter. "May I ask, Mr. May, what is the meaning of this ?" And Dehon brought the offending document close beneath May's nose, lying upon his chubby palm ; and then slapped it violently with his other hand.

"Of this ?" said May, innocently. "What is it ?"

"That, sir, is a letter I found among my wife's effects." And beyond all question the letter was in May's own hand-writing. May stared helplessly at Dehon ; and Terwilliger glared fixedly at May. And through all the embarrassment of the situation loomed up May's consciousness, antagonistic as their meeting was, that he was uncommonly glad to see him.

"Is—is Mrs. Dehon with you ?" said May, feebly, as the awful possibility occurred to him that they had been divorced.

"My beloved wife is in heaven," said Dehon, pulling out a large pocket-handkerchief and sinking back into his chair.

" My dear sir," cried May, grasping both his hands, " I am—unfeignedly sorry to hear it. When did——"

" That, sir," cried Terwilliger, furiously, "is no answer to my question. Did you, or did you not, write this letter ? " And he jumped from his chair and smacked the letter savagely against the dinner-table.

Evasion was impossible. " I am afraid, Mr. Dehon, that I did." Dehon fumed. " And now, my dear sir," said May, his face unconsciously broadening to a smile, "will you not stay and dine with me ? I have only——"

But at this the peppery old gentleman positively sailed off the floor in his passion. In vain May told him that he had received nothing from the late Mrs. Dehon but a long course of snubs ; in vain May assured him that he himself was more delighted than ever Mr. Dehon could be, that there had never been a possibility of his marrying the lamented Gladys ; it was to no purpose that he besought him to stay and dine. He tried to sympathize with Terwilliger in his loss, and Terwilliger grew only the more in- furiated. He pointed out to him that his letter had been entirely contingent, to take effect solely upon Mr. Terwilliger's death ; but upon this the old gentleman fairly choked with rage.

Finally poor Austin gave it up. He abandoned all effort to pacify him, and listened submissively to the philippic the indignant Terwilliger poured forth. And, to use the expressive but inelegant phrase of the day, he blew himself off right well. Austin sat and listened with a mind at peace.

A man's own eloquence is a great relief, and there is no knowing how far Mr. Dehon would have cooled off in time. It is possible that he would have ended by staying to dinner. But, just as he was finishing a most effective exordium, the noise of carriage-wheels was heard outside upon the gravel.

In two strides May was at the window, had thrown open the sash with a crash that shivered all the glass, and hurled himself through it into outer darkness, leaving the astounded Mr. Dehon, one eloquent arm extended in the air, addressing himself most earnestly to the four Copley portraits and the two battle-pieces of indigestible fruit.

V.

BEYOND all question this was now the
Comtesse Polacca de Valska. She was the
only one left. All others were present or
accounted for. Again May gained his pavilion, with the fleetness of an Exmoor deer ;
it was quite dark by this time, and he could
run about fearlessly. With a trembling hand
he adjusted his dark-lantern, lit the lamp, and
fixed the focus full upon the house-front
door.

He was just in time to see a veiled and
much beshawled lady assisted down from
the vehicle that stood at the door ; and after
a word of colloquy with the driver, she entered the house. May could not see her
face ; but it was just the figure, he fancied,
of the Countess de Valska. The carriage
drove away, the front door closed, and all
again was silent, save the thumping of poor
Austin's strained and shaken heart. Great

heavens! he complained to the harmless
Venus of Milo. The worst had been realized indeed.

This time there was no indecision. The
only safety lay in flight. When it came to
the point of marrying the de Valska, he
would be damned if he would. No sooner
had he gained this conclusion than he
sought to put it in practice. With quick
and stealthy steps he gained the stable. A
drive of fifteen miles to Framingham would
put him on the New York train; and the
Umbria sailed on the morrow. Little diffi-
culties with countesses were better understood on European shores.

But alas! it was only to find that the
stable-door was locked. He could hear inside the noises of a restless horse, but both
fast horse and buggy were beyond his reach.
The over-cautious Schmidt had locked them
in, and taken the key. May's heart sank.
He looked around for an axe, a log, anything to batter down the door with—he
would have set fire to his own stable if
necessary; then a brilliant thought occurred
to him—of the pistol-shot that was to be the
signal to Schmidt in cases of emergency.

He ran back to the pavilion. As he passed the house he thought he heard sounds of angry collocation in the entry. But this was no time for idle curiosity; and he ran on to the pavilion, grasped the revolver, ran back before the house, placed himself in the little clump of pines, and fired. The noises in the house ceased. He fired again.

The second report of his revolver was followed by a wild and shrill screaming in the house. A second after, the front door was violently flung open, and Mr. Terwilliger Dehon burst forth with the celerity of a pellet from a pop-gun. He was immediately and closely pursued by a female figure, screaming violently. After her, all in the focus of the dark-lantern, appeared a gaunt and stooping individual with a shotgun, which he brought to his shoulder and incontinently fired, aiming, as far as May could judge, at the North Star. Then he threw away the shot-gun and joined in the pursuit; and after him came the faithful Schmidt, in obedience to his master's signal, once more unperturbed.

"What has happened?" cried May, rushing forward. "Where is she?"

But even as he spoke, feminine arms were thrown around his neck, a fainting feminine figure hung about his shoulder, and feminine lips whispered in his ear:

"At last!"

With a gasp of despair, May disengaged her and led her to the front door, where he deposited his precious burden upon the china garden-seat. The countess seemed less graceful than of yore, and she certainly was heavier. But the countess, of course it was.

"Sech a time, Mr. May," said she. "Me a-comin' up with the dépôt-man, and findin' a burglar in the house; an' the volleys from the ambushes as was outside; an' Mr. Eastman a-runnin' for his gun, an' I chasin' the burglar; an' all along of that furriner in the kitchen as left the cellar-door wide open; an', says I——"

"Mrs. Eastman!" cried May, with a sigh of relief, as if he saw the dawn again. But that heroine's short-lived valor was exhausted. To chase an elderly burglar out one's own front door, amid salvoes of musketry, was surely excuse enough for leaning on the shoulder of the first reliable male one

met and knew; but the thought of both
actions was too much for feminine nerves,
and Mrs. Eastman proceeded to get up the
best notion of hysterics her Maine training
could produce. As for May, he was so glad
that it was not the Polacca de Valska that
he could have kissed even the elderly housekeeper; but he thought better of it, and
consigned her to the tender soothing of her
husband.

"Mirandy," he heard Mr. Eastman say,
"don't ye be a fool!"

Scene Fifth

THE RESIDUARY BEQUEST

I.

MAY went back again to his pavilion. Great heavens, what a day! He looked at his watch. It was already after ten o'clock; and his heart gave a leap of joy. Could it be that the countess would never turn up at all?

He was too much shaken by the excitements of the day to sit still quietly, and count the minutes; so he took to wandering in the drive-way about the lake. He was conscious of a marvellous accession of spirits! Poor Mr. Terwilliger Dehon! And May laughed to himself as he pictured their meeting, and the Eastmans taking him for a burglar. What could she have done to drive Dehon in such terror from the house? May wondered what had become of him, and looked with some apprehension lest he should have rushed into the lily-pond.

9

But that was impossible in so light a night. Moreover, he could have waded out. Well, well! he never should have known how to get rid of him. Peace to his widower's weeds.

The harvest moon had risen, and shone brightly on the familiar fields. Beauty is only relished by the free. How strong and sweet is our memory for places! Each swell of grassy hill seemed like an old playmate; the very contour of the masses of elm-foliage, darkly outlined under the moon, seemed all familiar to him. Every time that May walked by the main gate-way, with the iron cannon-balls, he looked nervously through it; but the white, shady road was clean and empty, and the night was still.

His fortune was almost too great to be believed in, and he looked frequently at his watch, and listened timidly for every sound. Had the countess forgotten him? Had she captured another? Well, Gladys was dead, and Georgiana "was married;" and he sat there, "dipping his nose in the Gascon wine" —still seven years short of "forty year."

But the night waxed and the moon rose higher, and the white mists began to drift in, stilly, from the distant river ; and there was yet no manifestation of the Countess Polacca de Valska.

And at last the village church rang out twelve bells ; and the cocks crew ; and May pitched his cigar into the lake with a sigh that resembled a benediction. The day was over. That most terrible twenty-four hours of his life was safely passed. He could go to bed and sleep serenely, in the conscious- ness that no one of his idle old dreams was to be realized, that no folly of his past was to assume shape and confront him now. And all his arsenal of weapons, his labora- tory of drugs, his store-house of Dutch courage, had proved unnecessary.

He walked along by the margent of the little lake ; and as he did so, a thought struck him. He entered the pavilion and set the fountain playing, in celebration of his deliverance. He threw open all the shutters and the wide door—useless precau- tions now—and the flood of moonlight streamed again into the familiar old hall. He looked about at the misanthropic pict- ures, and the moonlight fell fair upon the beautiful Venus of Milo in the corner. He looked again at the old will, and Georgiana Rutherford's note, and Mrs. Dehon's visiting-card lying beside it. Through such various fortunes had he tended into Latium.

He patted Fides on his massive head, as the dog walked along beside him. He went back into the house. It was all his own now; all his own, and untrammelled. He called his valet to him.

"Schmidt," said he, "I am not going to sit up any longer. If anyone comes, I have been here and gone—you understand? I have gone—to Arizona." Schmidt bowed. He had regained his imperturbability, and was fearful of being discharged. An American servant would have left, and brought an action for his ducking; not so the obsequious Oriental. And Austin May took his candle and went quietly to bed. He had kept his tryst honorably; he had made due tender of himself; and by all laws, human and divine, his three offers of marriage had now expired.

II.

A PRIOR MORTGAGE.

OUR hero sank comfortably into the great old-fashioned bed, with a sigh of relief that he could sleep at last in peace. The broad windows were opened, and the moonlight lay across the lawn; and from it came the speech of insects, and of summer birds; far off, one whip-poor-will.

If anyone ever deserved sleep, he thought that he did; but this is not a world where we get our deserts. All night long he lay awake. His mind would go from his infatuation with the de Valska to his passion for poor Gladys Dehon; from the Exmoor hounds to his engagement with Miss Rutherford. He was devoutly thankful that he had escaped them all, and yet the peace he had expected did not come. He heard the familiar old church-bell strike two, and three, and four, as he had heard it in his boyhood, when wakeful for a fishing-excursion, or for some country ride. What was he to do next?

He could not analyze his state of mind. The night hours passed, and still he lay there wondering. The whip-poor-will had some time been silent; suddenly, as if at a wave of an unseen baton, the orchestra of day birds fell to singing. May listened ; in eleven years he had not heard them. Then, as suddenly, they stopped. And then the dawn came, one ray of orange sunlight, and the fragrance of the new-born day.

At last he rose, impatiently, and went to the wide window. The sunbeams slid beneath the arching elms and slanted through the sward. Such scenes had been wont to make him happy when he was young—and when he was in love. This was a strange mood for him at thirty-three and free—a mood of melancholy, almost a loneliness.

Even his cold bath failed to restore him. He was glad they had none of them come ; he was certain of that. And yet——

As he was dressing, he opened the closet door. There was the broad straw hat, with its pink ribbons, still hanging, faded, on the nail ; and suddenly he recognized it. He

took it down, and looked at it curiously ;
and as he sat there, holding it in his hands,
the great St. Bernard dog came up and
sniffed at it. It was May Austin's. And as
Austin sat there, he remembered that he
had loved her.

He walked out upon the lawn again,
brushing the dews upon the grass. Fool
that he was! First loves were best, after all.

But where was she ? He had not heard
from her for years. He had never even
written, after the Trouville episode. And
she—she must have divined that he was
false. First loves were best. Oh, cruel
Uncle Austin! Yet his own wretched
fickleness was the most to blame, after all.
His uncle was a cynic ; but he had been a
young man in love.

Of one thing he was sure—though he had
taken eleven years to find it out. Wherever
she might be, throughout the world, there
he would find her. And he knew now what
had been in his mind, that yesterday, when
he had walked beside the lily-pond, along
the soft path no longer trod by her. Where
could she be ? First loves were best. And
he fell into a reverie.

He was still holding the hat in his hand,
and Fides came up again and sniffed at it.
There was something in his mouth—was it
a glove ?

May took the glove, and almost thought
he recognized it.   It was a woman's glove,
a garden-glove with a long arm—where had
he found it ?

The dog looked up at him, almost as if
he read his thoughts, and then he led the
way and Austin followed.   He went across
the lawn, and through the hedge, to the
well-remembered seat in the orchard, by the
linden-tree, and there he stopped.   And
May sat down upon the seat and dreamed.

An hour he sat there, and then he saw a
figure coming through the field.   And his
heart told him that this was May Austin.
She did not see him, and he waited there.

When she came out from under the last
apple-tree, he saw her stop and waver.   She
was lovelier still than he remembered her,
and he went up to her and took her hand.
She blushed, and he could feel it tremble as
it lay in his.

" I—I thought you were abroad," said she.

" I have come back," he answered, simply.

III.

THE POSTHUMOUS JEST.

An hour later Schmidt was sitting by the front door, smoking his long pipe, when he thought he saw his master crossing the lawn along the lily-pond. But he was walking hand in hand with a young lady. The long pipe dropped from Schmidt's hand ; and

" Potztausend ! "

The imperturbable valet was moved to say as much as this, but of further speech remained incapable. May approached.

"Schmidt, you will go to town and get the rest of my luggage."

The valet only stared.

"And after this I shall not need your services. I will find you a good place (with some of my bachelor friends," thought May ; " poor devils ! "). Schmidt still stood there, his broken pipe upon the door-step.

" Do you hear what I say ? "

Schmidt made an effort. "There is a letter for monsieur—in the pavilion." A letter! May trembled to himself once more.

"I must go home," said May Austin, still blushing violently. She lived in a cottage there, near by, that she had bought with her slender fortune. But May begged her to wait until he had gone to the pavilion, and then he would go with her. He feared that he knew what the letter was. But it had come too late! A thousand countesses could not bind him now.

Coming thither, May sat upon the doorstep, and Austin opened the letter.

LAW OFFICES OF VESEY & BEAMES,
3 COURT STREET, BOSTON,
August 14, 1886.

AUSTIN MAY, Esq., Brookline, Mass.

DEAR SIR : The eleven years' delay required by the will of your late uncle, John Austin, having expired to-day, I have much satisfaction in sending you a copy (herein enclosed) of the document contained in the sealed envelope referred to in said will, and constituting his residuary legatee ; although, as I am informed that you have never married, the residuary clause of the will does not take effect. The executors hold themselves in readiness to deliver over to you all the securities and titledeeds representing your uncle's estate upon receiving from you an affidavit that you have not, up to date, contracted a legal marriage.

I have some embarrassment in speaking to you of another aspect of this case, and can only hope you will think I acted for the best. You will remember that immediately after your uncle's death, I sent you a copy of the will as it was filed for probate. But when it came to a hearing I found that the court utterly refused to allow probate of a will which contained as a most important part the contents of a sealed letter, left in my custody, and the purport of which was unknown to the court. His honor intimated that he considered the will ridiculous in tenor and inartificial in structure ; and that it was at least questionable whether the residuary devise was not void, as dependent upon a condition in restraint of marriage. It was in vain that I cited the case where a man chalked his will upon his own barn-door, and the barn-door having been brought into court and copied was allowed to be replaced upon its hinges. The court wholly objected to being made, as it were, a confidant of Mr. Austin's love projects ; and insisted that the sealed letter should be opened then and there, and read to the court, and appended to the will and filed away with it. Accordingly this was done.

But I conceived that I should be best following out the wishes of your uncle and my old friend by not telling you of this. Suspecting that it would never occur to you to inspect the court records, the reporters were paid for their silence, and although you might at any time during the past eleven years have read this sealed envelope, your

continued absence abroad leads me to hope that you have
never done so.

    I am, sir, with great respect,

                Faithfully yours,

                        J. VESEY, JR.

Austin May dropped the letter from his
hands and looked at May. "I might have
known it any time these eleven years,"
said he.

"Known what?" said she, picking up
the enclosure, which had fluttered to the
floor.

"Perhaps it is as well," gasped Austin;
and he shuddered as he thought of Mrs.
Terwilliger and the scheming Countess.
He took the paper from May's hands and
read as follows :

"I, John Austin, gentleman, hereby incorporate this sealed writing, referred to in
my will of even date herewith, as part of
my said will. Having provided in such my
will that in the event of my said nephew,
Austin May, becoming married before he
attain the age of thirty-five, or before the
period of eleven years shall have elapsed
from the date of my death, whichever shall
first happen, all my property, real and per-

sonal, except my said bin of Lafite claret,
shall go to my residuary legatee ; and having observed a certain tenderness existing
between my said nephew, Austin May, and
my said niece, May Austin, I hereby nomin-
ate and create my dear niece, May Austin,
as such my residuary legatee—in the hope
that as I, marrying without love, have been
unhappy, they, my said niece and nephew,
marrying for love alone, giving up all
thoughts of worldly advantage, may enjoy
the blessings of this world besides."

The paper slipped from Austin's hands.

" To think that I have waited eleven
years ! " said he. And he struck his hand
against his forehead.

But May Austin looked up to him and
smiled.

.   .   .   .

Of the Countess Polacca de Valska, Austin never heard. Terwilliger Dehon re-
married, and, for the second time, a very
pretty woman ; such men always do. The
Burlington Quincys have also been married ; and Tom Leigh has come to stay at
Brookline for this season ; and Mrs Eastman's reign is ended ; but Fides is an hou-

ored inmate of the Brookline house. And if you drive by there, some summer afternoon, you will note once more about the windows those frilled and pleated things that denote the presence of a woman's hand.

THE END.

www.ingramcontent.com/pod-product-compliance
Lightning Source LLC
Chambersburg PA
CBHW021133020726
47500CB00003B/1057